W9-ANR-016

Miss Janis, . . . I came home only long enough to take you to my mother, before returning to Salisbury.

Some vague warning penetrated Crystal's brain. *He thinks he's master of all he surveys.* "Mr. Sutherland," she responded, trying but failing to sound as formal as he. "We haven't talked. I know nothing of your expectations. How do we know I'm even capable of fulfilling them?"

Spearing Crystal with the icy shards of his eyes, Adam spoke to Jessica. "Is this the reliable, competent nurse you promised me, Miss Cliburn?" he asked reproachfully. "I accepted your recommendation and had decided to try her, sight unseen. Instead, I get this lovely little dimpled blond who can't make up her mind. Apparently, this has all been a waste of my time."

With that, he turned on his heel and marched out the door.

Openmouthed, Crystal glanced around helplessly, hoping someone would come to her defense. When there was only silence, she rushed outside after him. "Mr. Sutherland, wait! Please don't blame Jessica. I *am* a competent nurse. I'll go with you if you need me."

His eyebrows lifted, and he squared his shoulders, gazing past her toward the distant Umtali Mountains. "Two minutes, Miss Janis," he granted in his clipped speech, as if doing her a great favor. "Two minutes!"

YVONNE LEHMAN lives in the heart of the Smoky Mountains and has four children. In addition to being an inspirational romance author, she is also the founder of the Blue Ridge Christian Writers Conference. *Drums of Shelomoh* is her eighth published novel.

Don't miss out on any of our super romances. Write to us at the following address for information on our newest releases and club information.

Heartsong Presents Reader's Service
P.O. Box 719
Uhrichsville, OH 44683

Drums
of Shelomoh

Yvonne Lehman

Heartsong Presents

To Vickie and Deon
For sharing their African adventures
in Rhodesia (now Zimbabwe)

ISBN 1-55748-409-0

DRUMS OF SHELOMOH

Copyright © 1993 by Yvonne Lehman. All rights reserved.
Except for use in any review, the reproduction or utilization of
this work in whole or in part in any form by any electronic,
mechanical, or other means, now known or hereafter
invented, is forbidden without the permission of the publisher,
Heartsong Presents, P.O. Box 719, Uhrichsville, Ohio 44683.

All of the characters and events in this book are fictitious.
Any resemblance to actual persons, living or dead, or to
actual events is purely coincidental.

PRINTED IN THE U.S.A.

one

Africa!

Smoke rose, spiraling upward from a bed of fire. Drums throbbed beneath the pulsing beat of shadowy hands. Deep black jungle thickened with foreboding rhythm.

The medicine man, face painted and feet bare, danced upon glowing coals. Gyrating feverishly, he thrust forth a doll, its long, silvery hair streaming about its face in wild disarray. Wrapped in a familiar scarf, the doll had been stabbed by a pin in the vicinity of the heart. The man spoke . . . and the only intelligible word of the entire proceeding became her name—

"Crystal!"

Crystal Janis bolted up in bed, raking her silver blond hair back from her face, now ashen with fear. Her blue eyes burst open as she struggled in the twilight zone between sleep and wakefulness, and she swallowed the scream that had formed in her throat upon seeing her friend, Jessica Cliburn, standing there.

"Jess!" Crystal gasped, gulping air and trying to calm the throb of drums resounding in her head and thumping against her chest.

"Wake up, sleepyhead!" Jessica tugged at the sheet. "We have a continent to conquer, you know."

Crystal shook her head. "I must have had a nightmare."

"Tell me about it," Jess said, perching on the side of the bed, "in twenty-five words or less."

5

Crystal laughed. In the light of day, the nightmare suddenly seemed no more than a silly dream. "It was nothing really." A rush of adrenalin returned the healthy glow to cheeks punctuated by deep dimples. "It was some kind of ritual, I think, complete with a medicine man—"

"Some kind of prophetic vision, you mean, Crys," Jessica announced with a crow of triumph, "and have I got a man for *you*!" Her dark eyes flashed. "Believe me, he's just the medicine you need."

"Men!" scoffed Crystal. "They're the *cause* of heart disease, not the *cure*." She was over Stuart now. But like a patient remembering pain, she had not been able to shake off the poignant reminders of what they had shared. To cover her confusion, she grabbed a pillow and threw it at her friend.

Jess caught it deftly. "No time for pillow fights," she said. "Mum and Dad insist on meeting you before they leave for work, so let's don't take time to dress. I'll go throw on a robe."

After Jess's quick exit, Crystal stood at the open window, gazing out upon a few scattered umbrella-shaped trees, a cluster of two-story white frame houses, and the infinite jungle beyond, bathed in the yellow-gold of early morning sunlight. In the distance, birds called and whistled, their songs as unfamiliar as the language she had heard only in snatches since coming here.

Below, at the end of the brick patio, a gardener's trowel scraped against a rock. The odor of moist earth and some unidentifiable sweet fragrance wafted up to scent the air. A bee droned lazily past the window.

Reassured by the serenity of the scene before her, Crystal shrugged away the unpleasant dream, undoubtedly conjured up by jet lag and her arrival on the Dark Continent in the dead of night. After picking her up at the airport, Jess's Land Rover had wound along dirt roads that twisted through the shadows, amid primal screams and screeches coming from the surrounding tangle of trees and lush undergrowth. They had reached the Cliburn home in the wee hours, creeping upstairs for a few hours' sleep.

Now Crystal's fair skin awakened under the splash of cool water and her eyes shone with the excitement of being so far from all that was familiar. She brushed her teeth hurriedly, then ran a comb through her hair until it hung in a shining fall of silk. After slipping into a kimono, she joined the Cliburns in the breakfast room.

It was like greeting family as she shook hands with Jessica's dad and embraced her mom. The distinguished William Cliburn was wearing a dark blue business suit and conservative tie, while Clara Cliburn's sunny yellow dress exuded as much warmth as her personality. They were the very image of success, more like a couple on their way to Wall Street than to a mission hospital in deepest Africa.

"I should have dressed, Mr. and Mrs. Cliburn," Crystal began on an apologetic note. "Sorry I'm so dowdy—"

"No, no, my dear," Clara protested. "You could never appear dotty to us."

"Mum," Jessica interrupted with a laugh. "It's 'dowdy,' not 'dotty.' You know, like . . . underdressed."

They enjoyed a chuckle together, admitting that their respective accents would take some getting used to. From her association with Jessica in nursing school, however, Crystal had expected the elder Cliburns' clipped British speech.

A cinnamon-colored woman entered with a newspaper,

a pot of coffee, and cups on a tray. Before the first sip, Jessica's parents were insisting that Crystal call them by their first names.

"As we mentioned many times in our letters," William said sincerely, "Clara and I were more than grateful when you and your parents took Jess under your wings during her nurse's training in the States."

Crystal dimpled at the comment, noticing how like her father William appeared when he reached for the paper.

"Now that Crystal's finally here, and we have two years to catch up on, I hope she can stay all summer," Jessica confessed, her face animated with pleasure.

"Sorry, Jess." Crystal gave a rueful grin. "I'm afraid my work at a nonprofit clinic did not make me independently wealthy. A three-week vacation was all I could manage."

"Oh, I think we can work out that little problem."

Seeing the mischievous gleam in Jess's eyes, Crystal was almost afraid to ask. "What's . . . worked out, Jess?"

"A job," she said, spreading her hands. "There's a temporary job available, and you'd be perfect for it."

Crystal's immediate thought was that there must be an opening at the Well Baby Clinic at the mission station in nearby Sanyati, where Jess had worked for the past two years. When her friend paused to clear her throat, however, Crystal knew that coffee wasn't the only thing brewing. So was trouble!

Jess smiled semisweetly. "Adam Sutherland will come by the mission to determine whether or not you're suitable, of course. But I know he'll like you."

William Cliburn lifted his silver head from his paper. "Suitable, dear? For what?" he asked his daughter in a tone that Crystal felt sure would wither even the indomitable

Jessica.

True to her prediction, Jess lowered her eyes before his stern gaze. "As temporary nurse for his mother while Annette Phillips is in Salisbury," she explained in a small voice.

William's snort and the way Clara clasped her cup with both hands spoke volumes. "Really, Jess!" her mother exclaimed indignantly. "You don't mean you would subject your friend to the likes of Etta Sutherland!"

"Well, Mum," Jessica replied defensively, "it's an emergency. Mrs. Sutherland needs someone with her while Annette and Adam are both away. And who knows—" she spread her hands—"this could turn into something permanent." She smiled at Crystal. "Then Crys can stay in Africa indefinitely."

"Adam Sutherland has been trying to find permanent help for his mother for the past eight years," Clara reminded her daughter. "Working for Etta Sutherland would be no vacation!" Her eyes darted toward Crystal and back to her daughter. "Not to mention . . . *Adam* Sutherland."

"But Crystal's a *blond*."

"You've been listening to gossip again, Jessica," admonished an exasperated Clara, who pushed back her chair and stood. "If there's a shred of truth to it, that's all the more reason to forget this preposterous notion of yours."

William gave up reading the paper, folded it and placed it on the table, then stood beside his wife. "Come by the hospital sometime today, Crystal, and we'll see what positions are available."

Crystal knew that when a hospital administrator makes

such a statement, a job is a near certainty. Somehow, though, it didn't stir her interest like Jess's "preposterous notion."

"Thank you, William," she replied gratefully. "But Jess has aroused my curiosity. I'd like to hear more before I decide." A hospital job might offer security, but Jessica never ceased to offer excitement.

Clara looked at her watch. "My rabbits are waiting, so we're off, darlings."

Jessica had already told Crystal about her mother's position as a nutritionist at the hospital in the capital city of Salisbury. And that she had been experimenting with raising rabbits for the much-needed protein lacking in the diet of most Rhodesians.

"What's this about being a blond?" Crystal asked as soon as the Cliburns had left.

Jess leaned nearer and dropped her voice, as if whispering would justify telling a rumor that might be better left untold. "You see, Adam Sutherland was desperately in love with a beautiful blond who ditched him. Since then, it's said he is trying to find her in every blond he meets."

Crystal fixed her friend with a stern look. "Jess, I don't intend to be a substitute for anyone's ex-fiancée." Then, in spite of herself, her dimples deepened. "Jessica, the matchmaker," she accused, remembering their college days. "Actually, you were rather good at it, as I recall."

"Oh, forget Adam Sutherland," Jess replied with an airy wave of her hand, and Crystal wondered how one went about forgetting a person one had never met. "About the job, Crys. Mr. Sutherland is really in a bind. And I just thought—" She looked sheepish. "That is, I sort of . . . recommended you."

"Sort of?" Crystal laughed. Jess never did anything halfway. A slight uneasiness nagged at her. "But your parents' reservation is surely not unfounded, Jess."

"Not entirely," Jess admitted. "Eight years ago, when Mrs. Sutherland's husband died in the same accident that left her an invalid, she became a bitter, disagreeable woman. The doctors told her there was no reason she couldn't walk again. But she wouldn't even try, and now is apparently unable to do so. And a couple of years ago, she became so despondent she even made a suicide attempt."

"Then you definitely need someone who is better qualified than I," Crystal said skeptically.

Jess disagreed. "Actually, she only needs someone to perform minor nursing services and act as a companion."

Crystal contemplated the offer briefly, then shrugged. "Well, at least I won't say no until I hear what Mr. Sutherland has to say."

"In that case," said Jess, pushing her chair back from the table, "you and I had better get to Sanyati. I want you to meet my Robert and—" she paused, a mischievous smile tugging at the corners of her mouth—"well, you may be surprised what Rhodesia has to offer."

Crystal grinned. Here she was in exotic Africa with her dearest friend and already with the possibility of a job that would allow her an extended vacation. But there was still something about the Sutherland case that bothered her.

"Why does the Sutherlands' nurse suddenly need to leave? Did something unexpected happen?"

"Happen?" Jess assumed an attitude of wide-eyed innocence. "Oh, something is always happening at Shelomoh. People are hired, fired, unable to cope with

Etta Sutherland's venom . . . or come under Adam Sutherland's spell—"

"Spell?" Crystal blazed. If she'd had an ounce of British cool, she would have lost it. "Who is this man, anyway? A witch doctor? Maybe there was something to that nightmare, after all." Determined to ignore the little shivers playing up and down her spine, Crystal drained her cup. "Anyway, if I don't like this Adam Sutherland when he interviews me, I can walk away. Right?"

"Right," Jessica echoed, but Crystal recognized that look in her eyes.

Jess always reminded Crystal of the Fourth of July—as if a giant fireworks display was about to erupt at any moment. She only hoped she wouldn't be caught holding a roman candle . . . with no place to throw it!

By midmorning, the canopy of space overhead was watery blue and virtually cloudless when they struck out for Sanyati Mission in the Land Rover. Only a few fading jet contrails smeared the sky like paint that needed stirring. It was more than an hour before Crystal noticed that the streaks had acquired a grayish cast and were hanging low on the horizon.

They had dressed for the weather—shorts, sleeveless shirts, and sandals—after Jess's early-morning weather prognostication: "Hot and humid!"

"Surely no hotter than the concrete sidewalks of Chicago," countered Crystal.

"Different. Our rainy season is almost over, though some of the rivers are still swollen. But it's terribly dry here from June till October."

Crystal thought of a thousand other contrasts as she

looked over the passing terrain. Instead of wide freeways with congested traffic, screaming sirens, and the odor of gasoline, there was a narrow dirt road snaking through a jungle of trees and vines, accompanied by the sounds of flapping wings and the smell of moist humus.

For some time they traveled along what Jess described as a "country road," but to Crystal appeared more like an abandoned path full of potholes.

"To our left is the Ingiati River," Jess pointed out. "It's a raging torrent in the rainy season, but it's already receding and in a few weeks will be only a few small puddles." Then she pointed to the east. "Looks like you're going to get a sample of our downpours, though."

Crystal fastened her eyes on the clouds in the far distance. They seemed to be rolling up the blue sky, exposing the under side, fast deepening to an angry black.

"Tell me about Robert," she asked quickly, eager to divert her attention from the ominous weather.

Jess was more than willing to fill her in on details about the surgeon whose wife had died of cancer several years before. As she spoke, the glow in her eyes revealed that her feelings for him were anything but casual.

"It's the real thing this time, Jess?"

"I love him, Crys. More than I ever thought possible." Their eyes met and held before Jessica returned her gaze to the road. "What happened to change your mind about Stuart?"

"I'm not sure. I thought I loved him, but when he asked me to marry him, I just couldn't—"

There was no time to finish her thought. Dead ahead, a big diesel van crammed with Africans, some clinging to the top, was careening down the path toward them.

two

"Oh, no! Hang on!"

Jessica swerved the Land Rover, tipping it precariously on its left wheels, finally coming to a stop between two trees, spaced barely wide enough for passage. The bus roared past, leaving behind an acrid smell, flying dust, and several new potholes.

"Are you all right?" Jess asked breathlessly.

"I think so." Crystal felt the spot where her forehead had made contact with the dashboard. "It's just a bump. But I thought wild *animals* was the problem in the jungle."

"As you can see, the real danger is wild *mankind*." Jess backed up and maneuvered the Land Rover onto the road, proceeding at a slower speed. "There are so few vehicles around that we never expect to meet anyone else." She tried a laugh, but Crystal knew the experience had shaken her, too.

"Should I call the Sutherlands when we get to Sanyati?"

Jess shook her head. "When Adam Sutherland is ready, he'll let you know."

Before Crystal could voice her opinion of such obvious chauvinism, Jess turned in to a remarkably Americanized village, built on a level stretch of land. "Sanyati has everything," she reported with pride. "Hospital, school, church, shops, laundromat—most of the comforts of home, in fact. A few miles down the road is a landing strip for small planes. The bush pilots land there when they

14

bring in the sick and injured."

Jess parked beside the hospital—a long, low white building with a flat roof. "We'll meet everybody first, then go to the apartment." She looked at her watch. "I timed it so we would be here for lunch."

They walked along a paved sidewalk, where several dark-skinned people sat on a low brick wall bordering the hospital lawn. Others, waiting for visiting hours or to see a doctor, stood under the overhang just outside the main door.

Jess greeted some of the people, using the thick African dialect known as Shona, then led the way into the building. "We have to close down for lunch," she told Crystal. "Otherwise, we'd never get to eat."

"Apparently, you're even busier here than we were in Chicago."

"We're at a greater disadvantage, too. We can't get supplies as readily here. And the people in the far villages have trouble reaching us."

Jess led the way down the hall and into the cafeteria. Quite a few green-smocked doctors, nurses, and other hospital personnel were already eating lunch. Seeing her, some of them lifted their hands in greeting.

"Eat up," Jess instructed, leading Crystal to a stack of trays. "We may have to resort to our own cooking for dinner."

They made their selections in the line, then walked over to a long table where two men were already seated.

"Allow me," said a male voice from behind.

Crystal looked around to see a young man dressed in casual slacks and sport shirt. With a slight bow, he took the tray from her hands. She looked over her shoulder at

Jess, who only rolled her eyes innocently.

The young man placed her food on the table, then set the tray aside, ignoring the chorus of chuckles from the others.

Crystal could hardly be offended. The guy was obviously a throwback to a more gallant era. The type who helped little old ladies across busy streets. Besides, he had such a pleasant face, complete with a scattering of freckles across the bridge of his nose. His definite masculine appeal was enhanced by a certain charming boyishness, complemented by reddish-brown, sun-kissed curls.

"Make it official, why don't you, Cliburn?" Golden glints twinkled merrily in his brown eyes.

"Crystal Janis, meet David Hamilton, a teacher at the secondary school," Jess obliged from across the table. "Crys is from Chicago."

"Hey, it's great to see someone from home!" He lit up immediately. "I'm from Missouri, practically next door."

"Really, David? What part?" Crystal asked, taking the chair he pulled out for her.

"St. Louis. But I've been all the way to Rockford, Illinois."

"Ah, world traveler," she quipped, watching David's disarming smile widen to a grin. "It's not every day I meet someone from down the road apiece."

"Don't mind us," spoke up a gray-haired man sitting across from David. His dark eyes, behind brown-rimmed glasses, held a hint of amusement. "Will someone please introduce us to the lady?"

"To be continued," David promised Crystal, then did the honors. "Dr. Emil Kent, chief administrator of the hospital, and Dr. Robert Braden, general surgery."

Robert's serious countenance and intelligent conversation befitted a successful, young surgeon. Crystal wondered if Jess was aware how often Robert's gray eyes sought hers, his expression unmistakably affectionate. Then, hearing Adam Sutherland's name mentioned, she turned her attention to Dr. Kent.

"Mr. Sutherland said he'd stop by on his way home from a business engagement to conduct the interview," he was telling Jessica.

Crystal couldn't help asking, "Any idea when that might be?"

Dr. Kent shrugged. "None. Though I must say, Miss Janis, I don't envy you that position, if you take it. My job running this hospital is a snap compared to dealing with Etta Sutherland."

"From all I've heard," Crystal replied truthfully, "I doubt that I'll get beyond the initial interview."

"Oh, after the glowing recommendation Jessica gave, I wouldn't be so sure. Still—" he lowered his head to peer over the top of his eyeglasses—"if you decide to accept the job, don't take Etta too personally. She doesn't allow anyone, with the exception of her son, to get close to her. Even I, who have at times prided myself on my patience and tact, have not been able to make a dent in that woman. Now I must get back to work." The older man rose and picked up a sheaf of file folders.

After he had left, Crystal looked around at sympathetic eyes and felt like saying to Jess, "Forget the interview and take me back to Salisbury."

But Jess was issuing an impromptu invitation. "If you guys don't have anything planned, how about dinner at our place tonight?" The suggestion met with instant acceptance.

"Hope that suits you, Crys," Jess said after Robert left to make rounds and David returned to school to meet his afternoon classes.

"Fine with me. Just give me a couple of hours. Besides an acute case of jet lag, I need to scrape off this layer of dust and shampoo my hair."

"Done."

When they stepped outside, Jessica seemed unconcerned about the blackening sky. "You like David, don't you?"

"Of course, who wouldn't?" Crystal eyed her friend with a knowing look. "So *that's* what you meant when you said, 'Rhodesia has much to offer?' "

Jessica smiled mysteriously and gestured toward the mountains far in the distance, almost obscured by the roiling clouds. "Beyond that range, over a hundred miles from here, are the Umtali Mountains. That's where the Sutherlands live."

"What's it like?" Crystal was both curious and apprehensive.

"I've never been to Shelomoh—that's what they call the estate," Jess explained. "But Dr. Kent says it defies description. It's far from civilization, on the edge of the deep jungle really. I suppose that only adds to the mystique."

Before Crystal could voice an opinion, she heard the drone of an approaching airplane. "Looks like one of your bush pilots is making a landing."

"So is the rain!" Jess commented, as huge drops struck the ground with the force of someone throwing darts at a target. "Let's go!"

They jumped into the Land Rover as people crowded

close to the hospital walls. Others moved under the thick trees.

The sudden cloudburst was so blinding that Crystal wondered that Jess could see to drive. On the way to the apartment, however, she managed to point out the school where David taught and, farther down the road, the row of apartments where she lived. Jessica turned into one of the attached carports, which offered some protection from the now torrential downpour.

"It won't last long," Jess called nonchalantly. "Come on." And she led the way inside, through a compact kitchen with dining alcove, and down a narrow hallway. "You'll have your own bedroom, since my roommate has gone back to the States. In here."

The small room Jess showed Crystal was neat and clean, though it did not particularly reflect the vivacious brunette's personality. Two curtained windows looked out on the distant mountains, while a single bed spread with a patterned afghan repeated the deep blues and golds of a fringed rug thrown over the hardwood floor.

Crystal kicked off her sandals and flopped on the bed. "Very nice."

"A little better than a college dorm, at least. Now I'll leave you to nap. You can unpack later."

When Jessica closed the door softly, Crystal sighed. Who was this Adam Sutherland, and why did she suddenly dread the thought of an encounter with him? Tracing the rivulets of water streaming down the windowpane, her eyes grew heavy, and she slept.

At seven, feeling rested and refreshed, Crystal and

Jessica greeted the two men. As the evening unfolded, conversation was light and easy, and Crystal's feeling of well-being increased. David had complimented her on her magenta outfit—shorts covered by a knee-length skirt and matching top—but he seemed equally interested in her ideas on a variety of subjects. She relaxed and began to enjoy the evening.

"My compliments to the chefs!" raved Robert at the conclusion of the meal, kissing his fingertips. "Spaghetti has never tasted so good." But his smile was for Jessica, a smile as warm as the one last piece of garlic bread he couldn't resist.

Crystal saw that look and couldn't repress a twinge of longing. Would she ever know that kind of devotion from a man? When David suggested a game of Monopoly, she was grateful for the diversion.

"This is about as close as I'll ever get to high finance," he admitted as he and Robert set up the board and divided the money.

Just then there was the sound of an airplane overhead.

"That must be Adam Sutherland," Jess said. "If it had been a bush pilot, he would have revved his engines to alert the ambulance crew to meet him." Her eyes widened. "Crystal, I'll bet Mr. Sutherland has come to fetch you."

"Me?" Crystal squeaked. "He couldn't. Not at this time of night."

Jess made a face. "When Adam Sutherland summons, you don't ask what time it is."

"Why? What kind of tyrant is he? Surely you people don't just jump when he speaks." Shocked, Crystal looked from one to the other in disbelief.

"Unfortunately, Mr. Sutherland isn't a believer," Rob-

ert tried to explain. "In our mission work, we have to begin
with people where they are. With the sick, we minister to
their physical needs before we can expect them to listen to
anything we have to say about Jesus Christ. With Adam
Sutherland . . . well, it's a little more complicated." He
paused. "He gave the mission station a second plane and
built a new wing on the hospital, so we try to cooperate
with him whenever possible."

Crystal nodded, understanding. "Sounds to me like he's
trying to *buy* his way to heaven." But she had the sinking
sensation that if Mr. Sutherland offered her the job, she'd
be letting them all down if she didn't accept.

The Monopoly game continued, and David made a
move on the board. "Looks like you're about to lose a hotel
on Boardwalk," he teased Crystal.

"Oh, David!" she wailed, playfully grasping his fore-
arm. "Just when I rise from the slums of Chicago to the
skyscrapers of New York, you take it all away!"

David opened his mouth to reply, but before he could
utter a word, a deep-throated British accent sounded from
outside the screen door. "I see I arrived just in time to
rescue the fair maiden."

All heads turned to observe the entrance of a man whose
imposing presence instantly dominated the room.

Stunned, Crystal could only stare. Nothing Jessica had
told her about Adam Sutherland had prepared her for his
physical appearance. Tall, commanding, the man was
wearing a dark business suit and tie, the interesting planes
and angles of his face accentuated by a shock of black
wavy hair. The strong jawline suggested unrelenting
sternness, while his first words had hinted at a sense of
humor. Whoever, whatever else he proved to be, Crystal

knew that here was the most fascinating-looking man she had ever met.

"Oh, Mr. Sutherland!" Jess said, jumping up to welcome him. "We didn't hear your vehicle. Please come in."

Crystal felt her color rise as his glance swept over her and lingered on her hair, then took in the hand still resting lightly on David's arm. She withdrew it and turned to give Jess a "Why didn't you tell me?" look.

"I believe you know Robert and David," Jess was saying as the two men stood and Adam stepped forward to receive their handshakes. "And this is Crystal Janis," she continued, as if presenting some sort of prize.

Crystal rose from her crouched position over the Monopoly board, smoothed her hair back from her face, and extended her hand. He grasped it firmly as she gazed up into eyes that might be anything from the dark blue of ocean depths to the inky black of outer space. His expression was speculative, but his handclasp was warm.

He spoke formally, with a touch of impatience. "Miss Janis, I'm sorry to ask you to accompany me this late in the evening, but I've been involved in meetings all day. I came home only long enough to take you to my mother, before returning to Salisbury."

Some vague warning penetrated Crystal's brain. *He thinks he's master of all he surveys.* "Mr. Sutherland," she responded, trying but failing to sound as formal as he. "We haven't talked. I know nothing of your expectations. How do we know I'm even capable of fulfilling them?"

Spearing Crystal with the icy shards of his eyes, Adam spoke to Jessica. "Is this the reliable, competent nurse you promised me, Miss Cliburn?" he asked reproachfully. "I accepted your recommendation and had decided to try her, sight unseen. Instead, I get this lovely little dimpled blond who can't make up her mind. Apparently, this has all been a waste of my time."

With that, he turned on his heel and marched out the door.

Openmouthed, Crystal glanced around helplessly, hoping someone would some to her defense. When there was only silence, she shook her head and rushed outside after him. "Mr. Sutherland, wait!" She caught his arm as he reached the Land Rover. "Please, don't blame Jessica. I *am* a competent nurse. I'll go with you if you need me."

His eyebrows lifted and he squared his shoulders, gazing over her head toward the distant Umtali Mountains. "Two minutes, Miss Janis," he granted in his clipped speech, as if doing her a great favor. "Two minutes!"

three

"Two minutes!" Crystal fumed, tossing clothes into suit-cases only recently unpacked.

"Maybe you shouldn't go," Jess said, a thoughtful expression on her face.

"And let Adam Sutherland think you and I are completely irresponsible?" Crystal continued to stuff makeup into a zippered case.

"You don't have to prove anything to that man. You see what a beastly person he is."

"Well, I can see that he thought he was hiring a competent nurse and, instead, he thinks he's getting a 'lovely little dimpled blond, who can't make up her mind!'" Crystal mimicked him, and they laughed uneasily.

"Then maybe you *do* need to prove him wrong."

Crystal paused long enough to look Jess in the eye. "If I can handle the problems in Chicago, I think I can handle Adam Sutherland and his mother," she said with more confidence than she felt. "Anyway, you said he'd be away on business, and if Etta Sutherland doesn't like me, I'll call, and you can send a replacement."

"That's the spirit!" Jessica cheered her on. "But remember, he has this thing for blonds. So watch your step."

"Really, Jess. I don't have to reciprocate, you know."

"Famous last words," her friend retorted. "He's not the average man, Crystal, so be careful."

24

"And I'm not a child, Jess. Surely, Mr. Sutherland can understand plain English."

"Righto! Plain English, British English, Bantu, Swahili, Shona, and who knows how many other languages!"

"Fine." Crystal pretended to be unimpressed. "Then I'll simply tell him where I stand."

Jess groaned. "That's just the problem. Women don't *stand* around Adam Sutherland. They *swoon*."

Crystal ceased her packing to stare at Jessica in disgust. "If Adam Sutherland is such a blond-snatcher, why on earth did you volunteer *me* for the job?"

Jess sighed. "I did it because I felt sorry for the Sutherlands, I suppose. Besides, it's only a couple of days and the job pays well. In no time, you'll be back, and we can pick up right where we left off."

In spite of her irritation, Crystal couldn't help smiling at the sight of her friend sitting on an overstuffed suitcase, struggling heroically to snap it shut. "I know you mean well, Jess. And don't worry about me losing my head over Adam Sutherland. You know I prefer a nice, wholesome guy."

"Like David," Jess finished for her.

"Possibly," she returned noncommittally.

"I knew you'd like David. Maybe you'll marry him and stay right here in Rhodesia."

"Oh, no!" Crystal groaned, hearing the engine of the Land Rover catch. She grabbed her purse and the makeup case. "My two minutes are up!"

"One last word of advice," Jess said, dragging the suitcase to the door. "Etta Sutherland can't abide wimpy people. Stand up for your rights. She'll respect you more if you do."

Crystal knew she needed a full indoctrination on the Sutherlands, but it was far too late for that now.

David picked up the luggage and followed her outside. He thrust the bags into the back while Crystal slid in beside Adam Sutherland. Hands on the open window frame, David bent his head to speak to her. "Thanks for the dinner. We'll have to do it again when you're not so . . . rushed."

With a jolt, the Land Rover moved forward, gaining speed. Crystal looked back and waved, then braced herself as Adam swung onto the rutted dirt road.

"When did you arrive, Miss Janis?" he asked after a moment or two.

"Late last night, I think, or early this morning. I—I guess I've lost track of time." She gave herself a mental kick for stumbling over the answer to his simple question. "It *is* Wednesday, isn't it?"

"Yes. And this is the last week in May," he said, as if reciting the months of the year to a kindergartner. "Do you think you'll enjoy your stay in Africa?"

Crystal wasn't about to let this infuriating man keep her from it. "Oh, I'm sure I will. After all the concrete of Chicago, I'm delighted to see so much vegetation."

There was a brief pause. "You obviously made quite a hit with David Hamilton."

She detected an edge in his voice, though she was probably mistaken. Britishers were sometimes hard to read, she'd found. "It's amazing," she went on. "We're almost neighbors back in the States. And we have so much in common. Seems I've known David all my life. Sort of like the boy next door, you know."

"No, I wouldn't know," he objected. "Next door to me

on one side is the jungle, on another the copper mines. Then there are the irrigation projects and the valleys—"

"Your world is quite different from mine," she acknowledged.

He nodded in agreement, then cast a glance in her direction. "Are you disturbed about something?"

"Disturbed?" she asked innocently, trying not to grimace as the Land Rover plowed over the dirt road, bouncing her up and down as if on a trampoline. "Just because you haven't missed a pothole yet!"

"Pothole?" He frowned. "Perhaps when the rainy season ends, the mission station will get around to correcting the deplorable road conditions."

Crystal bristled inwardly. She certainly hadn't intended to imply that the mission was responsible for his lousy driving! How could two people who spoke the same language fail so miserably to communicate? They hadn't gotten off to a very good start, but she could at least be civil.

"It's just that I'm still a little shaken over the close call Jess and I had this morning," she explained.

"Close call?" He furrowed his brow in confusion.

She laughed. "Another Americanism, I'm afraid. We were forced off the road." She told him about the van and, when she had finished, he shook his head.

"Who was driving?"

"How would I know?" she asked, puzzled.

His broad chest expanded with the deep breath he drew. "You said you were in the Land Rover. Surely you know who was driving," he said with exaggerated patience.

"Oh, I thought you were asking who was driving the bus." She looked at him warily. "Does it matter?"

His dark eyes narrowed. "I understand *Americans* drive on the wrong side of the road."

She could not resist a rejoinder. "At least, in America, our roads are wide enough to have more than one side." But when he swerved, she got the feeling he was trying to hit the pothole rather than miss it!

Suddenly the landing strip came into view and he lurched to a stop. Grabbing her suitcases, Adam ran for the plane.

She raced to catch up with him. "Why bother with a plane, Mr. Sutherland?" she yelled. "We were flying in the Land Rover!"

"Must you fight me all the way, Miss Janis?" he muttered under his breath as she reached up and hoisted herself onto the single step and into the small craft that seated three in addition to the pilot.

She was tempted to turn back, but in no time flat, he had stashed the bags in the back, crowded into the pilot's seat, and closed off her only way of escape.

"I had expected a level-headed, poised professional, someone who could rise to a difficult occasion," he began, as he fastened his seat belt. "In a matter of a few minutes, Miss Janis, you have managed to destroy any illusion I might have had about American nurses."

"Computerized robots may be a thing of the future, Mr. Sutherland," she replied stiffly, "but all the nurses I know *currently* are human beings."

"Are you implying I treated you less than that?"

She determined not to spar with him unnecessarily, nor be inhibited by him. "You weren't exactly cordial."

Adam inhaled sharply. Then, turning his attention to the controls of the plane, he executed a neat turn and sped down the runway. Soon the small craft had lifted off, leaving the mission station far behind, and leveled out to skim the African landscape.

"It's so light outside!" Crystal exclaimed, hoping that their conversation might lighten up also. "Almost like day."

"Yes, the moonlight is brilliant here," he explained. "Without that, and a knowledge of my direction, I could not fly at night." He gestured toward the stretches of flat land across the plateau. "One can even play tennis by the light of the moon."

"Do you play?" she asked, wondering if such a busy and important man ever engaged in anything so ordinary.

He swiveled his head of silky dark hair, beautifully cut, to regard her. "A few years ago, when I was in college," he said, and Crystal realized he was younger than she had thought. Maybe midthirties. The silvery moonlight softened the contours of his face, and he appeared more relaxed here, soaring through the night sky. "Do you play?"

"I play softball," she murmured, looking out beyond the nose of the plane.

"Softball?"

She put her fingers together and made a circle. "You know, a ball about the size of a small grapefruit."

"Yes, I know." He scowled slightly, facing straight ahead.

Feeling they had nothing in common, Crystal looked out the window on her right. Soon she was mesmerized by the scenery—softly rolling land, lushly green, silvered by the pale rays of the moon. Excitement stirred in her veins. There were elephants and lions and other wild and beautiful things down there. She wanted to see them all.

How strange. She had been in Africa for only twenty-four hours, yet here she was with a man she barely knew, on her way to some unknown destination. Jessica was right. So far, Rhodesia had been full of surprises. Feeling a sudden shiver of apprehension, she dropped her head, her hair swinging forward to veil her face.

"Perhaps I've been abrupt," Adam admitted. "It's just that I'm in a bit of a hurry. After my meeting in Salisbury tomorrow morning, I must fly to London for some important government negotiations. My mind had been at ease about my mother until I came to fetch you, and you indicated your uncertainty about accepting the position."

Just as her spirits lifted to think this man might actually be apologizing, his mood changed. "I'm afraid I don't take lightly the wasting of my time."

"What a pity, Mr. Sutherland," Crystal said, resenting the implication that his feelings were the only ones to be considered. "I only hope it is not a waste of *mine*."

His lip twitched, and she got the distinct impression that he was resisting the impulse to laugh. "Jessica Cliburn told me quite a few intriguing facts about you."

Crystal watched him warily. *Intriguing* was hardly the word she would have chosen to describe her activities in the slums of Chicago for the past two years.

His voice dropped, and his dark eyes flashed as he looked over at her once more. "I must say I had to see for myself whether your hair was truly the color of . . . moonlight on the veldt."

She squirmed beneath his appraising glance, feeling like an ice cream sundae waiting to be consumed. Was he thinking of the lost love Jess had mentioned?

Disconcerted, she crossed and uncrossed her legs, realizing with a start how she was dressed. Did he think she had deliberately worn these clothes to be provocative? No wonder he hadn't perceived her as a thorough-going professional.

She tugged at her shorts and made an effort to smooth them against her legs. *Get hold of yourself, Crystal,* she scolded. There were reasons for the unaccountable tension that had flared between them. People's inner problems often caused them to behave erratically. And she had to admit *she* had been prejudiced by Jessica's admonitions. Maybe she should try to understand, just as she would if Adam Sutherland were a patient of hers.

He definitely had a problem with hair color. "Being blond is important to you, Mr. Sutherland?" she quizzed in what she hoped was her most professional voice.

"A definite advantage," he replied. "Can you imagine what it is like to be constantly surrounded by dark skin, dark eyes, dark hair? The Africans are a beautiful people, mind you. However, in this culture, blonds are a rare treat, the exception. Your eyes are blue, are they not, Miss Janis?"

"Baby blue," she admitted reluctantly.

"No. Fire blue. Like a flame at its hottest point, as if something inside is smoldering."

"It's this cabin. It's suffocating in here." She reached for the neck of her shirt and fanned herself.

"Forgive me if I've made you uncomfortable, Miss Janis. I'm merely trying to see you through my mother's eyes. I'm sure she would find someone of your delicate coloring quite pleasing indeed."

She glanced at him from the corner of her eye, hoping

he couldn't hear the thundering of her heart over the roar
of the engine. She considered his explanation, but recalled
that it wasn't his *mother* who was rumored to be looking
for his fiancée in every blond he met.

"Look down," he said suddenly, as he began circling a
mountain range. "These are the Inyanga Mountains. The
lower ones are the Umtalis, which surround my estate. The
Umtali village is located in the valley."

His excitement was contagious, and she took in the
majestic peaks, the shimmering ribbon of river winding
through the floor of the valley below.

"And there is my home—Shelomoh." He spoke with
pride, and Crystal could sense his deep love for it.

She unfastened her seat belt and leaned toward the
window for a better look. The main house was a massive
English-style Tudor, with gabled terra cotta roof. Two
wings enclosed an expansive courtyard. Mirroring the sky
was a rectangular swimming pool, almost as big as the
tennis court on a level below it. Beyond the pool stood a
row of small cottages, their red roofs and white exterior
matching that of the manor house.

Manicured hedges sectioned the estate into neat squares
running across the top of a mountain that had been leveled
to accommodate the sprawling enclave. At the front of the
house, beyond the flower gardens and sweeping lawn, was
the jungle, sloping toward the valley below.

Knowing he was waiting for her evaluation, Crystal
turned her face toward him. "It looks—" she
breathed—"like Camelot, almost too beautiful to be real."

He seemed to be studying her face, then cleared his
throat. "Then perhaps your brief stay at Shelomoh will not
be too unpleasant."

"Shelomoh," she repeated, looking down at the spectacle spread out before her. "What does the name mean?"

"It means 'peaceable'," he replied. "My father built the estate and named it for a reference to King Solomon's own kingdom. Historians report that King Solomon had gold mines in Rhodesia, and since my father made the major portion of his fortune in gold and copper mining, the name seemed appropriate."

"And is it? A peaceable kingdom, I mean?"

A shadow crossed Adam's face, and his scowling silence confirmed the problems Jess had alluded to. "Mother is a complex woman." When he didn't pursue the subject, she wondered if that would be his final answer. Then, "Fasten your seat belt. We're going down."

four

The treetops rushed up to meet them as the plane nosed down toward a narrow landing strip.

"Mother's nurses have never lasted very long," Adam said. Then, as if guessing Crystal's unspoken question, he added, "I must warn you that my mother may appear rather difficult—even hostile."

"And I must warn *you*, Mr. Sutherland, that I am a nurse. Not something to be snarled at nor eaten alive."

He exhaled audibly as the wheels of the plane touched down on the single runway, and the trees on each side streaked past. "Knowing my mother's demanding personality and having witnessed your defensive attitude, I can only conclude that this position would be an inconvenience for you, though I'm sure your friend, Miss Cliburn, had only the best of intentions in recommending you."

Crystal gasped. What had happened to the tenuous thread of understanding that had begun to develop as they explored his jungle kingdom together? What had she done to make him believe she was unsuitable to care for his mother?

"Mr. Sutherland, I have never received anything but praise concerning my professionalism. But," she said accusingly, "I suppose that anyone who judges a prospective employee on the basis of hair color is bound to be disappointed in other areas."

The only indication that he had heard her was a slight

34

twitching of his lips as if he found something humorous. "You have only to ask, and I shall return you to the mission station this very evening, Miss Janis. Dr. Kent should be able to find someone with a stronger constitution, someone whose ... *social* life ... won't be at risk."

With fists clenched tightly at her sides, her eyes smoldering with blue fire, she lifted her chin defiantly. "If you think I am going to back out now, Mr. Sutherland, you have another thing coming! I'm no quitter! I accept the position! Now, if you want to fire me, that's your prerogative."

"Not a chance, Miss Janis," he said, bringing the plane to a smooth stop and sitting back to gaze at her with satisfaction. "You've just passed the interview with flying colors!"

"What interview?"

"Oh, you've been under observation from the moment we met. The first test was to determine how you would react in a crisis. After all, Miss Janis, a person can stop breathing in the space of two minutes. Don't you agree?"

She looked at him aghast, not knowing whether to laugh or cry.

Without another word, Adam Sutherland reached back for the luggage. Then, opening the door of the cockpit, he hopped to the ground to greet a tall, lanky man getting out of a metallic-gray car parked near the runway.

Adam handed him the luggage, then moved aside to introduce them. "Miss Janis, George Coleman. George manages the estate in my absence."

"Good evening, mum." George's British accent should not have come as a surprise to her. "All is well at the house, sir," he said, turning to Adam.

Adam acknowledged the remark with a nod. "Will you take Miss Janis's luggage to the nurse's suite, George?"

"Yes, sir." Retrieving the bags, George swung them effortlessly at his sides as he walked toward a Land Rover at the far edge of the runway.

"Now, Miss Janis, are you coming, or have you changed your mind again?"

Adam reached up for her, spanning her small waist with strong hands and setting her on her feet on the ground. She had expected to jump down on her own, and told herself that's why his unexpected action took her breath away.

She stood for a moment, inhaling deeply of the cool night air, and looked out toward the jungle. Perhaps it was the profound silence that struck her—the absence of traffic, emergency vehicles, voices. There were some strange night sounds, but they seemed very far away.

No, it was something else, something that reminded her of her dream. A vibration? There it was again! A throbbing like a low hum, almost like the beating of a heart. *Thrum. Thrum. Thrum.*

"What is that I hear?" she asked, cocking her head to identify the sound.

"Drums." He smiled at her benignly. "The tribes are announcing your safe arrival. Their drums are an amazingly effective means of communication, even in this electronic age."

"You're trying to rile me again, Mr. Sutherland." She was beginning to feel uncomfortable. "Why should my appearance here possibly be of interest to them?"

"My dear Miss Janis, 'riling you,' as you call it, seems to take very little effort on my part," he retorted. "But in answer to your question, it is always of interest when someone from the outside comes into their midst. And you are blond and fair—a novelty here, as I have already explained. Not only that, but you are a nurse, and if they have a medical need, they will seek you out."

She could not repress the sudden shiver of fear that rippled down her spine.

"But you're getting cold in this night air, and it's late. Shall we go ... home?" He handed her a ring of keys and slid into the passenger seat of the Bentley.

Crystal could not believe her ears. "You expect *me* to drive?"

"Just consider it another test. You may need to drive Mother in to Umtali while I am away. I thought perhaps you might enjoy getting the feel of the automobile." He settled back and folded his arms over his chest, regarding her with an expectant look.

She shrugged, accepted the keys, and slid in behind the wheel.

He explained the controls, and she eased the great car onto the paved road he pointed out. Gliding through the night, illuminated by the headlights, Crystal relaxed at last and listened as Adam Sutherland briefed her on her assignment.

"I've had the most highly qualified professionals tackle my mother's case, but I might as well have hired another paid servant to do her bidding—"

"Mr. Sutherland," Crystal interrupted, "with your unique manner of interviewing, it's no wonder you've been unable to keep help."

His face darkened. "That's only a sample of what you may have to endure from my mother." She heard the weariness in his voice. "But what she needs is communication and companionship, and that can only be experienced with a person of backbone, someone who will not simply defer to her every whim."

"I'm not sure I qualify," she replied skeptically. "This may be hard for you to believe, but I'm not in the habit of sparring with people, especially not with patients."

"You're right, it *is* hard for me to believe," he said in a mocking tone. "But we'll see what happens after you meet my mother. And I will understand if you don't feel you can stay. After all, the best of us have failed with her. My only advice is to follow your instincts."

She risked a light laugh. "Now that is something I've been trained *not* to do, Mr. Sutherland. Nurses are supposed to be precise, controlled, logical, and down to earth."

"Well, since we're in this together, let's at least dispense with formality. Please call me Adam."

Before Crystal could register the shock this announcement brought, he was directing her to make a left turn. It led to a paved lane separating the maze of manicured shrubs she'd seen from the air, and wound up to the house now visible on the knoll.

She followed his instructions to park under an enclosed carport where George was pulling away in the Land Rover. Adam explained that the caretaker lived in a cottage behind the house with his wife, who worked at a shop in Umtali.

A long ramp slanted up to the door. That would be for Mrs. Sutherland's benefit.

"Keep the keys," Adam said, "just in case." She put them in the pocket of her shorts.

Adam pressed a button outside the door, apparently

summoning the housekeeper, for as soon as he used his key and entered, a tall, dark-skinned woman in a bright floral dress and matching turban appeared at the far end of the hall and glided gracefully toward them.

He introduced the woman as Kudzai, who brightened when she saw him, then asked in limited English if she should rouse the household staff, who had retired for the night. When Adam waved away her question, the woman reluctantly turned her attention to Crystal.

"Tea? Somet'ing to eat?"

"Nothing, thank you," Crystal replied.

They walked past her on a brief tour of the house, and the tall woman stood stiff and erect, the look on her haughty face nothing less than unmitigated hatred. Crystal felt a cold, unreasoning fear. What reason would this woman have to dislike her? But if the drums had foretold Crystal's coming, perhaps they had also conveyed some other message.

She thought briefly about the near accident on the road to Sanyati. Had it been premeditated? She knew that foreigners were not always welcome, particularly when they represented an unwanted religion. And many of the natives held superstitious beliefs, trusted witch doctors, even practiced voodoo! She would have to ask Adam Sutherland.

Beyond the kitchen, at the left of the carpeted hallway, Adam pointed out an elevator that led to an alcove on the second floor between his mother's rooms and the nurse's quarters. Continuing on toward the front of the house, he led the way to the large formal drawing rooms. The glass panels on either side of the massive front door were covered by dark drapes. Paneled walls and heavy doors between the rooms guarded whatever secrets might lie behind them. Mahogany tables with fat legs squatted along the walls, holding lamps that poured forth no welcoming glow, but stood in the solemn shadows.

The house and its furnishings had the look and feel of great wealth, Crystal decided, but there was no light here, no life. Rather, the place reflected Adam Sutherland's darker side, when that moody, brooding look crossed his face.

Moving through the hallway once again, Adam took the wide sweeping staircase in the center of the house. Faint lamplight glowed from the landing at the top as they climbed the stairs. Crystal fastened her eyes on that, running her hand along the satiny mahogany of the railing. When they reached the top, she saw that the staircase continued up to yet another floor.

Opening the door into a sitting room, Adam stood back and Crystal stepped through. Glimpsing the bedroom beyond, she breathed a sigh of relief at the sight of the airy, well-lighted apartment with flowered curtains pulled back across windows running the entire length of the outer wall. Someone had set her luggage inside.

"The nurse's rooms," Adam explained. "Your bedroom is next to Mother's, separated by the alcove off the hall. Perhaps it would help to think of the house in the shape of an H. Your suite forms the upper right part of the H, which is at the back of the house, Mother's, the upper left."

"Has the nurse already gone?" Crystal asked.

"Yes, she said she would leave written instructions for you. Now I need to go and prepare Mother for your arrival."

When he left, Crystal discovered a bath located next to

the sitting room. She renewed her lipstick and ran a brush through her hair, wondering if Mrs. Sutherland would be offended by her casual attire. Then she reminded herself nervously that, based on everything she had heard, the woman would most likely be offended by her mere presence in the house.

Returning to the bedroom, she took time to look around. She had been vaguely aware of the grandeur of an era gone by, but now she took in the lavish details. The high ceilings. The elegant furnishings.

Running her hand along the polished surface of a carved lowboy, Crystal noticed a sealed envelope marked "Nursing Instructions." She opened it and took out a long thin chain with a key on the end, then began to read:

> *To Whom It May Concern.*
>
> *I'm so sorry to have to leave so suddenly, but I must see about my mother, who's in the hospital in Salisbury. The doctors say her tests don't look good. They've found cancer.*
>
> *Enclosed are instructions for Mrs. Sutherland's leg massages and medication. She does enjoy the whirlpool, but is very self-conscious about being observed, and prefers Bari, her personal maid, to help her with that.*
>
> *Her medicine is kept in a wall cabinet. Keep the enclosed key on your person at all times, as Mrs. S. attempted suicide a couple of years ago. The family—Mr. Adam and a daughter in London—are quite disturbed that she may try something like that again.*
>
> *I probably shouldn't be putting this in writing,*

since I don't know who may be reading this note, but
I think she's scared to death that they'll put her away
somewhere where she can't harm herself. Not only
would she lose control of the estate, but she thinks
her family has lost respect for her, that she's let them
down and can't be trusted. She's well aware that if
she doesn't follow her son's wishes, he will have no
alternative but to place her where she can be
watched.

Though I hate to say this, I'm worried about her,
too. Mrs. S. has always been outspoken, but lately
she's been more and more withdrawn. I'm not sure
that there's any medicine for that.

The nursing duties are simple and not even very
time-consuming. I wish you well and hope to be back
in the next few days—Annette Phillips."

Crystal refolded the note and whispered a prayer, re-
minding herself that there was really nothing to fear. Still,
she looked across the room to the wall of windows,
wondering what view lay beyond. Her impulse was to take
that route, the thought occurring that the drummers had
better keep their tom-toms warm to beat out the message
that Miss Janis had come and gone, all within a matter of
minutes!

Hoping to get a glimpse of the infamous Etta Sutherland,
Crystal tiptoed into the alcove that joined the two bed-
rooms. She stood, holding onto the doorcasing outside
Mrs. Sutherland's room.

Reflected in the mirror of a large antique dresser was the
image of an old woman, pale against the white pillows
propped at her back. Her eyes were closed, but her

expression did not appear relaxed, rather distressed. Her
white hair, brushed back severely, did nothing to flatter
her face, but drew attention to her nose and prominent
cheekbones.

A movement caught Crystal's eye, and she noticed a
dark woman in a green uniform standing by the bedside,
hands folded in front of her, as if waiting for a command
from her mistress. That must be Bari, the personal maid.

Even before meeting the patient, Crystal felt her inad-
equacy. Apparently Mrs. Sutherland had needs that the
finest professionals had been unable to meet. Including
spiritual needs that even the good Dr. Kent had failed to
fulfill.

What have I to offer her? Crystal asked herself. Her
professional experience had been among the poor and
outcast. Her personal background, middle-class and
conservative. Here in these opulent surroundings, she was
decidedly out of her league.

She fought the impulse to insist upon being returned to
the mission station. She had friends there. She knew what
to expect from them.

"Miss Janis," came a voice in her ear, startling her from
her reverie. Her eyes flew to the reflection and she
discovered Adam Sutherland towering behind her, staring
down at the top of her head.

He raised his hand . . . to touch her arm? to strike her?
An uncontrollable urge to escape so overwhelmed her that
she moved forward, stumbled, and caught her sandal on
the edge of the oriental rug covering the hardwood floor.
Horrified, she found herself plunging headlong into Mrs.
Sutherland's bedroom.

Suddenly she was lifted and pulled back against a taut

body. The muffled sound from the other side of the bed came from the dark-skinned woman who quickly covered her mouth with one hand, then lowered her head, the whites of her eyes barely visible as she peeked through narrowed lids.

Crystal was aware of the rise and fall of Adam's chest at her back, the hammering of his heart beating in rapid unison with her own. She felt like an animal, trapped by a big game hunter, as Etta Sutherland's accusing dark eyes took in the amazing scene. The painful moment seemed endless as they faced the woman, her brow lifted in surprise.

When she spoke, her words were laced with sarcasm. "Is this flaming-faced girl, who cannot even stand on her own two feet, the competent professional you hired to assist a helpless invalid, Adam?"

five

It wasn't likely that Etta Sutherland really considered herself a helpless invalid, Crystal thought. The obvious strength of her arms and upper torso, as she moved herself into a more upright position, served to confirm the remarks made by everyone who had discussed her case. No, Mrs. Sutherland's major problem was obviously not of a physical nature. Nor did she appear to be as depressed as Crystal had been led to believe. The proud lift of her chin and her penetrating gaze epitomized an eagerness for battle from one confident of victory.

"Mother, I'd like to introduce Crystal Janis," Adam said simply.

This time Crystal was grateful for Adam's strong arms about her, supporting her trembling knees. "How do you do, Mrs. Sutherland?" she managed.

The lamplight no longer shone on the woman's face, and the shadows created dark circles beneath her eyes and hollowed out her cheekbones, giving her a ghastly appearance.

"Hmph! She doesn't look a day over eighteen," Etta Sutherland snorted. Her eyes shifted to her son, still encircling Crystal's arms in a vicelike grip. "And she's a blond, I see."

Adam released Crystal at last, coughed lightly into his hand, and moved to stand at the foot of the large, four-poster. His eyes seemed to flash a warning signal to his mother before a smile touched his lips. "And a very attractive blond, don't you think, Mother? That should be a nice change for you."

Crystal hugged her arms to herself, feeling suddenly chilled. The warmth of Adam Sutherland's strong body, where she had stood pressed against him, had served as a shield against his mother's animosity. Now she felt quite alone and unprepared.

Her gaze dropped, and she uttered a silent prayer for guidance. She had come to Africa for a vacation, not to become embroiled in some complicated family drama. She was only a nurse. They needed someone trained in family counseling!

"She's Jessica Cliburn's age," Adam was saying. "You must know that Miss Cliburn is assistant director of the Well Baby Clinic in Sanyati. She's, um, twenty-five?" he probed, trying to draw Crystal into the conversation.

"Twenty-five in November."

"Do you realize, Adam, that she's forty years younger than I?" Mrs. Sutherland scoffed. "What on earth can this . . . *child* . . . do for me? We wouldn't even be able to communicate!"

Crystal felt Adam's eyes on her, a plea that she defend herself. No doubt he was wondering what had happened to her backbone. The least she could do was state her professional qualifications, her nursing experience, perhaps elaborate on her tact, diplomacy, and patience.

But to deliberately provoke a fight with this woman violated Crystal's deepest principles. And, facing facts, she knew Mrs. Sutherland's needs exceeded any of the skills she had to offer.

Looking neither at the patient nor her son, Crystal

sought out the maid standing in the shadows where she had retreated earlier. "If I can be of any assistance here, I'll be glad to stay."

"Oh, that really won't be necessary," said Etta Sutherland sharply, addressing her son. "I don't need a nurse. Bari can do for me and wear that key around her neck. She'd be much more capable of preventing my taking it away from her than this girl."

Self-consciously, Crystal reached up and fingered the chain hanging, blatantly, outside her shirt. The key was a symbol of Etta Sutherland's unforgivable indiscretion. A daily reminder. Like an albatross around her neck. Crystal realized that she should have had the forethought to tuck it out of sight.

In the uncomfortable silence, Adam's sudden announcement had the ring of finality. "Miss Janis stays."

Resignation veiled Mrs. Sutherland's eyes, and her face became a mask, as impassive as her voice. "Yes, Adam. I realized that was settled before you entered this room. I am well aware that my wishes are not the issue here. In fact, I should not be surprised if Mrs. Phillips does not return and your nurse occupies that room permanently." Her eyes darted toward Crystal as if she expected a denial.

Crystal's mouth opened to oblige, then promptly closed. It would be unwise to attempt a defense.

Adam, too, ignored his mother's remark. Impatiently, he looked at his watch. "I have an appointment, Mother. You'll have to excuse me."

"At this hour, Adam?"

He received the question as if it were a reprimand. "I can stay until morning, if you prefer."

"Why should I, Adam?" came her clipped retort. "I have

. . . your nurse . . . to look after me."

It was clear to Crystal that this episode in Mrs. Sutherland's bedroom was a charade, a farce, for each of them knew it was Adam Sutherland who made the final decisions. His mother had played the game, then ultimately conceded the victory to her son.

At that moment, the woman did not seem to be bitter, just defeated. How painful it must be, thought Crystal, for a person of such means and obvious spirit to be in subordination to her son. And Adam apparently did not recognize his mother's sarcasm as a cry for help.

A display of sympathy would be an affront to Etta Sutherland's dignity, so Crystal prayed for wisdom to handle the one slim chance remaining to win the woman's trust.

While she tried to think of what to say, Adam spoke up. "It's very late. I'm sure you want to get settled for the night, Miss Janis," he said with a gesture of dismissal.

"No, Mr. Sutherland," Crystal replied, her heart thundering against her chest at her presumption. "It would be against my professional and ethical standards to consider staying under these conditions."

Her resolve almost weakened under his icy stare, but from the corner of her eye, she saw Mrs. Sutherland watching her curiously.

A look of disbelief swept Adam's features. "Surely you aren't responding to that ridiculous insinuation!"

Chin high, Crystal met his gaze. "I have no choice, Mr. Sutherland. I have an obligation to consider the patient first. I cannot take the position against her wishes." She paused long enough to be sure she had Etta Sutherland's full attention. "I would be willing to take the job only if

Mrs. Sutherland herself makes the decision to hire me." She lifted the chain from around her neck and handed it to him, her eyes pleading for understanding.

He took the key and pocketed it with a sigh of impatience. "Then I'll return you to the station anytime you're ready, Miss Janis."

His voice was cold, and Crystal felt the bite of failure at his words. She closed her eyes and bit her lip. Now what would she do? Perhaps she should have just walked into Mrs. Sutherland's room, answered her questions like a professional, accepted Adam's terms, and hoped for the best after his departure. After all, she would have been here for only a couple of days.

She could hardly believe her ears when Adam spoke again. "That is, unless my mother decides to keep you on." He moved toward the doorway. "I believe there is tea waiting in the kitchen. Mother, I do hope someone will inform me of your decision sometime before morning."

He left the room without a backward glance.

Fearing that Mrs. Sutherland would think she had tried to manipulate the situation and would resent her even more, Crystal darted a glance in her direction.

The woman was staring, agape. "Well, that's a new one."

Crystal swallowed hard. "I thought it worth a try."

"Why?"

"Because," she began, cleared her throat, and started again, "because I believe you and I do have something in common."

Mrs. Sutherland's look was withering, but her silence encouraged Crystal to continue. "You see, before coming here, I lived with my parents in Chicago. They advised me, evaluated my actions, and questioned my every decision. It was done in love, of course, but sometimes I resented it, felt they should let me make my own mistakes."

Seeing that Etta Sutherland was listening, she went on. "I feel a similar situation exists here. Only in reverse. It is the son who makes decisions for the parent. He means well, of course, but . . . I can understand how you must feel."

The moment of surprise in Mrs. Sutherland's expression quickly passed. Something akin to a "Hmmmph!" escaped her lips. "You couldn't *begin* to understand how I feel." She rolled her eyes toward the ceiling. "Anyway, I've proved myself incapable of making proper decisions. It's only right that Adam take over."

"Then," said Crystal slowly, "let's humor him."

Once again, Mrs. Sutherland shot her a disbelieving look. "That's not the way it's done here, child. Everyone humors me, but obeys Adam."

"Not I, Mrs. Sutherland. I'm here on a three-week vacation. My friend recommended me to Mr. Sutherland as a companion for you while he's away on business. So, I'm not here to obey anyone. Only . . . to offer my services to you. If they're not wanted—"

"But shouldn't you be with your friend?" she interrupted.

Crystal shook her head. "Jess has to work until the weekend. Our visit can wait." She braced herself, but the expected onslaught did not materialize.

Rather, the woman's tone was one of resignation. "Two days, you say?"

"Yes," Crystal replied, feeling a strange sense of expectancy. "Only until Annette Phillips returns."

"And Adam is obviously eager for whatever late-night appointment awaits him in Salisbury—" Mrs. Sutherland paused, and Crystal let out a sigh. Apparently the woman had convinced herself that Crystal was not here for Adam's benefit. He had other plans. "You can read, I suppose?"

Crystal nodded. "Shall I . . . find a book?"

"For goodness sake, not another African history or how to cope with one's illness!"

Whether Mrs. Sutherland's decision had anything to do with Crystal personally, or was made solely for Adam's sake, Crystal had no way of knowing. Nevertheless, she could not contain the joy that bubbled up for the first time since arriving at Shelomoh, dimpling her cheeks.

Etta Sutherland took note of the dimples, then turned to the woman in the corner. "Bari, please tell Adam that I said goodbye. And I wish him well in his . . . negotiations."

Murmuring, "Yes, ma'am," the dark-skinned woman scurried out of the room.

"I'll find something to read," Crystal said, heading for the adjoining bedroom.

Elated with the small victory she had won in Etta Sutherland's room, Crystal was nevertheless drained from the tumultuous events of the past hours. Still, she relished this opportunity to get to know better the woman who had baffled the best minds. Quickly selecting a novel she had begun reading during the flight from Switzerland to Africa, she returned to her new employer's room.

Mrs. Sutherland didn't look nearly so foreboding now, only tired. "Are you still awake?" Crystal asked softly, moving an armchair nearer the bed.

Without opening her eyes, Etta Sutherland said, "Let's hear your opinion of my reading tastes. What's the book?"

"Oh, I chose one of my own, Mrs. Sutherland. It's a romance novel set in England during World War II. If we're going to spend time together, you might as well get to know the real me."

"Begin," the woman commanded.

Turning up the lamp and clearing her throat, Crystal began reading the first page.

She paused only when Adam's plane sounded overhead, seeming to dip toward the rooftop in salute. Was he pleased, she wondered, that his mother had allowed her to stay after she had openly defied him? But, she reminded herself, she was not here for his pleasure. She was here to care for his mother.

Etta Sutherland's eyes fluttered open, considered the ceiling, and closed again.

Crystal's voice was tiring when Bari brought in a tray prepared by Kudsai. Tea for two, accompanied by delicious flaky pastries with fruit filling. Apparently there was no restriction on Mrs. Sutherland's diet. Bari fluffed the pillows behind her head and asked if she could do anything more.

While they nibbled on the refreshments, Crystal sought some indication as to whether the older woman was enjoying the story. "Do you find a book set in wartime, depressing?"

Mrs. Sutherland gave the question a moment's thought. "No, although I lost a brother in World War II." A faint light shone in her eyes as she reminisced. "Those were fearful times. My Reginald was a bomber pilot, and my every waking moment was a prayer that he would return to me." Her voice took on a twist of irony. "It never occurred to me that he would be killed right here on his own property, in a *Jeep* accident."

What could she say? Crystal thought helplessly as Mrs. Sutherland replaced her cup on the tray and leaned her head back against the pillows. She picked up the book and began to read.

"That will be enough for now," said Mrs. Sutherland when she came to the end of the chapter. "You must be quite tired."

"A little," Crystal admitted. She placed a marker in the book and closed it. "I haven't had time to catch up on my sleep or become accustomed to the time change."

"You must be anxious to get back to your friend and begin your vacation."

"Yes, but there are two sides to the story. Jessica thought that if I had work, I could afford to stay all summer."

"So you *did* want this job?" Mrs. Sutherland peered at her intently. "And it was your friend who arranged it?"

"Yes," Crystal replied reluctantly, not wishing to discredit Jess. "But believe me, Jessica's intentions were only the best," she insisted, placing her hand impulsively on Mrs. Sutherland's.

The woman flinched at the touch. "And how do *you* feel about it?"

Crystal withdrew her hand and stood to put her teacup on the tray. "I think I could love it here in this house, in this beautiful setting—" She paused to look Etta Sutherland directly in the eye. "But I could never, under any circumstances, take a job only for the money. I must feel I'm needed, wanted."

"I'm sure we can find some use for you," Mrs. Sutherland replied stiffly. "For a few days, that is, until Adam and Miss Phillips return."

Crystal smiled. "Good night, Mrs. Sutherland."

Though Crystal's smile wasn't returned, a trace of color appeared in the woman's pale cheeks. "If I need anything during the night, I'll ring for Bari," she said, inclining her head toward a control with buttons on the bedside table. "And don't bother with the lamps. Bari will come in again tonight."

Excusing herself, Crystal went into the adjoining suite. Bari was there ahead of her, with her suitcase open, placing lingerie in a drawer. A vague concern crossed her mind that Mrs. Sutherland's personal maid might have reason to resent someone hired to be her mistress's nurse-companion.

"Oh, you don't need to put my things away, Bari," she said hurriedly. "I can do it."

In the light, she estimated Bari to be in her forties, a few inches taller than she, and about twenty pounds heavier. The woman had a pleasant round face and short hair arranged in an Afro style.

Hearing her come in, Bari turned and smiled. "No problem," she said in a soft voice matching the expression on her face. "I glad mistress let you stay."

Encouraged by her friendly overture, Crystal risked a laugh. "I almost ruined everything when I stumbled into her room, though."

Bari laughed, too, her eyes crinkling at the corners. "Mos' people, they pretend not be afraid of her. They talk to her like she baby. Or sick ol' woman."

"To tell the truth, I am a little scared, Bari," Crystal

confessed. "If you can tell me anything that will help me
understand Mrs. Sutherland, I hope you'll share it with
me."

Bari sighed. "Nobody know what to do no more." She
reached into her uniform pocket and brought out the key
to the medicine cabinet. "Mr. Adam, he tell me give you
this."

The two women smiled at each other. "Do you have a
family, Bari?"

Bari's smile faded. "My husban', he killed long time
ago. Mistress, she take me in, me and children, give me
job." Her face brightened as she added, "My little Lalani,
she stay here, help cook and clean."

"I'll look forward to meeting her," Crystal said sincerely, hoping she had made a new friend in Bari, who had
finished unpacking one of the suitcases.

They said goodnight, and Bari hurried back to Mrs.
Sutherland.

After putting away the last few items, Crystal slipped
into a robe, opened the doors leading onto the veranda, and
stepped outside.

The moon was still shining brightly, illuminating the
wooden banister, painted white, that stretched along the
back of the house and connected the two sections of the H.
Rimming the veranda were pots of flowering plants, ferns,
and small trees. White wicker tables and chairs, cushioned
with plump pillows, were positioned in conversational
groupings.

Sinking onto one of the chaise lounges, Crystal stretched
out, arms above her head. Drawing in a breath of the fresh
night air, she looked out over the railing. In the brilliant
light, the lawn shimmered as in a mirage. Water sparkled

in the swimming pool, reflecting the myriad stars above, and the trees cast lacy shadows on the ground.

Unaccountably dogs began to bark. Something flashed in the distance. What was that? She sat up to get a better view. A narrow beam of light caught her eye as it bobbed among the trees just past the pool. She stood and walked over to the banister, placing her hands on the ledge.

The strange light was still now. She felt a shiver of apprehension. Was she being observed by someone out there? The light moved on momentarily, disappearing behind the trees, and she shrugged away her anxiety. It was probably someone who lived in one of the cottages she'd seen from the air. Or George, making certain everything was secure for the night.

She heard the throb of distant drums. Were they spreading the word that she was staying after all?

Unbelievable, she thought, returning to her bedroom. She'd been in Africa for little more than a day, and already it was an experience to remember. How Jess would laugh about her bizarre introduction to Etta Sutherland.

Smiling, she crawled into bed and snuggled between the luxurious bedcovers. Even the drums were not disturbing now. Their rhythmic murmur was a lullaby, soothing her. She fell asleep instantly, and her slumber was deep and dreamless.

six

Crystal was awakened, later than she had intended, by the radio, tuned to a station playing native music. At least no witch doctor had stolen her away during the night!

Dressing hurriedly, she walked out on the veranda. The dazzling rays of the morning sun glazed the courtyard, the pool, the jungles of the Umtali Mountains, and the higher Inyangani, its crest swathed in cotton-candy clouds.

Looking down, she spotted Bari bringing a breakfast tray to a poolside table set for two, where Mrs. Sutherland had wheeled herself. The older woman was wearing a lavender quilted bedjacket, a plaid woolen afghan drawn over her legs.

Crystal took the elevator and joined them there, greeting the two women with a cheery "Good morning!"

Lifting her snowy head, Mrs. Sutherland did not speak but acknowledged Crystal's presence with a solemn nod, as if her appearance were somehow unexpected. "That will be all, Bari," she said, unfolding her napkin and placing it on her lap. "Everything seems to be under control here."

Bari gave Crystal a weak smile before turning to go back to the house.

Mrs. Sutherland seemed none the worse for her late-night activities, Crystal decided, noticing that her skin was remarkably smooth for a woman in her midsixties. The slight color in her cheeks did not appear to be fever, but good health. It was the dark circles under her eyes and her diffident manner that suggested stress.

Mrs. Sutherland gave a curt nod and reached for a frosted glass of fresh orange juice.

"I hope you slept well," Crystal said, drawing a small book from the pocket of her robe. "I thought we'd have our morning devotions together before we eat."

Etta Sutherland set her glass down on the table with a resounding crack. "The book you read from last night was entirely satisfactory. Introducing something new would only confuse me. I can't keep my mind on too many things at once."

Crystal recognized a lame excuse when she heard one. "Oh, this one isn't new, and it won't confuse you," she countered. "It's just a little reading about nature."

"The food will grow cold."

"It's covered."

Mrs. Sutherland again lifted the glass to her lips, and Crystal waited. She would not openly defy the woman. Finally she nodded, "Go ahead."

Crystal read a passage of Scripture, then a brief paragraph that applied the Bible truth to life today. Closing her eyes, she offered a prayer, thanking God for the beauty surrounding them and the friends she had made in Africa. She concluded by asking His blessing on the food and on her new employer.

"Hmmph! I suppose this little ritual makes you feel better," Mrs. Sutherland commented, taking the silver lid from the tray to reveal a steaming mound of scrambled eggs, hash browns, and plump sausages.

"I wouldn't start the day without it. I find I need it quite as much as food."

Etta Sutherland's dark eyes were piercing. "It's easy for you to sit there and thank God for everything . . . as long as you have it," she accused. The momentary pain changed to an expression of despair. "But do you know what it's like to lose someone you've built your whole world around?"

Crystal waited in silence while the older woman served her plate. "No, Mrs. Sutherland," she said at last, "I guess I can't imagine what it would be like since it hasn't happened to me. And the persons I dealt with in the slums where I worked never had much to lose."

The black eyes snapped. "Do you think for one moment, young woman, that I don't know you're trying to use something from some psychology book on me?"

"Why, no," replied Crystal, feigning surprise. "After all, didn't you say that you can't concentrate on more than one book at a time?"

Mrs. Sutherland acknowledged the verbal coup with a slight quirk of her lips, then lest the movement be interpreted as a smile, ordered gruffly, "Fill your plate. Before the food grows cold." Picking up her fork, she said, "Don't waste your time on me, child. It's all been tried before, by the old and experienced—doctors, psychologists, psychiatrists, former friends, Emil Kent. . . . Do you know him?"

"I've met him."

"That man has resorted to every possible argument, debate, coercion, but to no avail. I'm not even angry with God anymore." She picked up her knife and began to slice a bite of sausage. "That's supposing there *is* one, of course."

A phrase from Shakespeare crossed Crystal's mind.

Methinks the lady doth protest too much. No doubt Mrs. Sutherland expected her comments to be challenged. But what could be said that hadn't been said before?

With a sigh, Crystal plunged in. "Would you mind if I told you about some people I know?"

"If you wish," the woman replied blandly, lifting the bite to her mouth.

For several minutes Crystal related her experiences in the slums of Chicago—the deprivation and disease, the heartbreak of homelessness, the rare displays of courage and tenacity she had found among some of the destitute. "A few who had absolutely nothing were hanging on to the hope that one day everything would be all right."

Just as Mrs. Sutherland was about to throw down her napkin in disgust, Crystal delivered her parting shot. "Some of those people remind me of *you*."

Etta Sutherland's mouth dropped open, and Crystal pressed her advantage. "Despite everything you may say to the contrary, I detect a strong and indomitable woman who will never give up!"

The surprise in the dark eyes gave way to a misty sheen of tears before she dashed them away. "That's where you're wrong. I'm afraid it's too late for this old woman, Miss Janis."

Etta Sutherland was not angry, Crystal suspected. Poverty, despair, anger, disappointment, frustration, disease— all these Crystal had observed and tackled in the slums of Chicago. But indifference was a wall she didn't know how to scale.

"Please, at least call me Crystal. And may I call you by your first name?" At Mrs. Sutherland's questioning look, she explained. "In America, many women prefer to use their own first names. I suppose it makes them feel younger, more independent."

The older woman shrugged. "It won't make me feel any younger, but if you wish, you may call me Etta."

After Etta wheeled herself inside, Bari came out to gather the dishes and Crystal asked her about the day's schedule.

"The mistress, she watch television some mornings. Sometime she read. And sometime . . . she go to third floor."

"The third floor?" Crystal asked curiously, thinking Bari might be able to shed some light on this house and its occupants.

A sad look crossed the maid's round face. "Before he die, those rooms b'long to Mr. Reggie and the mistress. She 'low no one up there except to clean. In eight year, nothing change."

Crystal could not fault the woman for wanting to remember her husband as he had been, the days when they had been so happy together. Yet it seemed such a waste that she should continue to live in the past, never finding fulfillment in the present.

After Etta's midmorning exercises, Crystal wheeled the woman into the garden, where the flowers and shrubs were in fragrant bloom.

"How strange," she commented, walking over to a tree whose limbs resembled gnarled roots. It hadn't a single leaf or bud. "Will the leaves come later, or is it dead? Everything else is so green here."

Etta wheeled over to inspect the tree. "That's the baobab. Cream of tartar comes from them. Occasionally they might sprout a few leaves, but some never do. An African legend says that God got angry with the tree one day and pulled it out by its roots. When He put it back in the ground, He replaced it upside down. That's why the roots grow from the trunk instead of the branches."

"Are they referring to the God we believe in, or some other?" Crystal asked curiously, touching a rootlike limb that reminded her of driftwood.

"And what God is that?"

"The *only* God," Crystal replied stubbornly. "The One Dr. Kent believes in. The One *I* believe in."

"Mmmmm," Etta mumbled. "I wouldn't know. Many of the Africans believe in some other kind of god. One the medicine man conjures up. The kind associated with voodoo."

Automatically Crystal felt a chill and hugged herself, turning to gaze out at the mountains looming in the distance.

"What is it, Crystal?" Etta asked, following her line of vision.

"Oh, I'm sorry. I didn't mean to startle you. I was just remembering a strange dream I had when I first got here. It had to do with a medicine man . . . and a voodoo doll—" she glanced at Mrs. Sutherland, adding in a small voice—"one that looked like *me*."

"That could be a premonition," Etta said, turning the wheels of her chair toward the paved walkway. "Or a warning."

Crystal followed, moving closer. "What kind of warning?"

"Who knows? Strange things happen around here. I suspect Kudsai knows all about the voodoo. It works, you know."

"I don't doubt it," Crystal replied uneasily. "But fortunately, God's power is far greater than any other."

"Then it doesn't frighten you?"

"Of course not."

When they reached the courtyard, Etta wheeled over to the lounge chairs in the shade of the jacaranda trees, their lavender blossoms in full bloom. Crystal helped her out of the wheelchair and onto the lounge.

"Elise was scared silly," Etta said, looking up.

"Elise?" Crystal settled herself on the lounge next to Etta's.

"She was a blond, like you. Ah," she corrected herself, "not like you at all, but a beautiful girl nonetheless. She was always afraid of Africa, its dark people, its sounds, its voodoo."

Crystal's curiosity was aroused. She had the feeling this was the same blond Jess had mentioned. "Was Elise a friend of yours?" she asked carefully.

"A friend of Adam's. We all thought . . . well, never mind. Adam wouldn't like my discussing Elise with you. He's a very private person."

Crystal risked one further question. "What . . . happened to Elise?"

"She married. Her husband runs several corporations in Europe, and they live in London, quite near my daughter, as a matter of fact."

"Do you see her often?"

"Gwen visits once or twice a year. I have two grandchildren. When they were small, they accepted me totally, and after the accident, when I thrived on my grief, they were most sympathetic. Now that they're older, they have their own friends, their own interests. They're all angry with me."

"Why should they be angry?"

"The doctors say there is no reason why I can't walk. Apparently, I am the only person who knows I cannot." She gave a gesture of dismissal. "I can't imagine why I'm telling you all this."

Crystal felt a surge of compassion. "Probably because you feel I'm no threat to you. In a couple of days I'll be gone." Her voice softened. "Etta, you need to talk to *someone*. I hope you know you can tell me anything that's troubling you."

Etta shook her head. "There's really no point."

"What about your friends?"

"Ah! I ran them off years ago," she replied with a snort. Then her face crumpled, and she sighed. "I really tried at first. Reggie and I had so many friends, but I was suddenly a third party. An embarrassing one at that."

Crystal felt at a loss. How did one begin to help such a proud woman? "Can you tell me something about your injury?"

Suddenly Etta's expression was shuttered. "I don't want to talk about it further. This conversation depresses me."

At that moment, Lalani, a seventeen-year-old version of Bari, came out to say that Mr. Adam was on the phone.

"Come with me," Etta instructed Crystal. "He may want to speak with you."

Etta took the call in the library. Almost immediately, her voice became argumentative, and Crystal stepped into the hallway, though she could not help overhearing.

"But she's only a young girl, Adam. You should hear what she's been through for the past two years in those slums." There was a moment of silence. "Oh, Adam, this is no time for jesting. She's too lively to be stuck way out here with an old woman."

Silence again. Then, "Pleasant, Adam. A little saucy, but not disrespectful. Oh, now *there's* an idea. You can try, but . . . oh, all right. Goodbye, Adam."

Hearing the click of the receiver, Crystal returned to the room. "Is something wrong?" she asked, seeing the worried look on Etta's face.

"The exploratory surgery on Annette Phillips's mother revealed a worse condition than anticipated. The doctors could not operate."

"I'm so sorry." Crystal sank into an armchair across from Etta.

"Miss Phillips will not contact us again before Monday. Adam said that I should ask you to stay until then." She quickly added, "I told him that would be an imposition. That you're on vacation."

Crystal studied the pattern on the rug. It occurred to her why this was so difficult for Etta Sutherland. If she failed to retain Crystal as her nurse-companion, Adam would be forced to take other measures.

Etta gave her a speculative glance. "My son said you might consider staying . . . if we invited your friends here for the weekend."

"When will he be back?"

"Late Friday night or early Saturday," Etta replied, "but if you prefer to return to the mission station, Adam can take you then."

Crystal fixed the woman with a level gaze. "If *you* want me to stay, I will. It's only a few days until Monday. And I'll still have two whole weeks of vacation left."

Mrs. Sutherland seemed relieved. "Then I'll certainly make it worth your while financially."

"Oh, Etta!" Crystal cried in exasperation. "Don't you know I wouldn't stay for the money? I'll stay because I want to!"

Etta lifted her chin. "I don't accept charity from anyone," she said abruptly, and wheeled toward the doorway.

Crystal stood. "Does that mean you want me to leave?"

Etta's forward progress halted. "It means," she replied, without looking back, "that you have a job until Monday. However," she paused dramatically, "I insist upon your friends coming sometime this weekend."

After lunch, Crystal called Jessica and was astonished to learn that Adam had already contacted her.

"He said you would be asked to stay until Monday, and apologized for the inconvenience."

"And what did you tell him?" she asked her friend. Jess could be so exasperatingly long-winded.

"Well, I didn't want Adam Sutherland to think you were money-mad or eager to be cooped up in that jungle. A man like that would never believe it's out of the goodness of your heart that you'd put up with his mother! So, I told him the most difficult part was that you, being accustomed to an exciting social life, might get lonely."

Crystal couldn't hold back the laughter. Jess would never change! "And that's when you two planned a party?"

"No, no. Adam Sutherland thinks *he's* the one who thought of inviting us to keep you company. So we'll be waiting to hear from you with our party duds on! By the way, Crys, David wants you to call him. Got a pencil to take down his number?"

After ringing off with Jess, Crystal went to Etta Sutherland's room. "Would you like me to read to you?"

"I really couldn't concentrate," she replied listlessly, lying back against her pillows. "It's the Phillips situation. Another confirmation of the unfairness of life." She lifted her hand helplessly, rolled her head to one side, and closed her eyes.

Crystal gave Etta some medication prescribed for stress and depression. It would help her sleep. She returned to her own rooms, thinking how quickly one could become enmeshed in another's life.

Walking out onto the darkened veranda, she sat down in a chair, puzzling over the paradox of Etta Sutherland. If this were a permanent position, with time to know the woman better, she might be able to work out some plan that would be helpful.

Looking up, a flash caught her eye. Someone was at the edge of the jungle, just like the night before. Was it some ritual? She remembered Etta's saying Kudsai knew about voodoo. Did the dark-skinned native practice the pagan religion?

Crystal reprimanded herself for the thought. Just because Kudsai was wary and distant didn't mean she practiced voodoo. It could be anyone out there. That was not a comforting thought, and she returned to her bedroom and drew the blinds. Sleep did not come easily that night.

Friday dawned, bright and hot, a carbon copy of the previous day. Etta, however, was more subdued, and Crystal didn't attempt to engage her in conversation when she grew silent. It was natural that she should be concerned about the problems of Annette Phillips.

Only the mention of Adam brought a spark of life to Etta's eyes. "We won't see much of him," she said as they ate dinner together on the veranda. "But it's good knowing he's nearby. I worry that he is working too hard. Not only does he run this estate, but he must oversee the irrigation projects and participate in some government affairs."

"You're quite proud of him, aren't you?" Crystal asked softly.

Etta looked toward the distant mountains. "Without Adam, I would have nothing at all. Oh, sometimes I wonder how he feels. He never talks about it, but the accident changed everything for him. He and Elise—" She broke off. "Now why has Elise come to mind so often lately? I haven't thought of her in years. Of course," she said with sudden clarity, her glance falling on Crystal, bathed in the fading sun's golden glow. "It's your hair."

Crystal only smiled. "Shall I read another chapter?"

When Etta was asleep, Crystal called David, who was in the midst of grading papers.

"It's tough, Crystal," he said wistfully. "Knowing you're so near, yet so out of reach. But I know about responsibilities and commitment, too. We're all grateful to you for pitching in like this."

"Glad to help, David," she said, and meant it. "I may be here a few days longer than planned. Just until Monday."

"Is Adam Sutherland there?" he asked abruptly.

"No. He won't be back until late tonight or early tomorrow."

"I see. Well, Crystal, what can I say except I miss you? I wanted to get to know you right away, dispense with the formalities, you know."

She laughed softly. "We did that the moment we met, David. It was as if we'd always known each other."

"Yes, it was like that, wasn't it?" He paused before speaking again. "I'd better get back to my papers before I say too much. But I get the feeling that you and I understand each other, Crystal, even without words."

"I think you're right, David." She told him about the possible plans for the weekend. "So, I may see you sooner than you think."

"Great!" His voice was suddenly charged with excitement. "In the meantime," he added huskily, "dream of me."

"Good night, David." She replaced the receiver, smiling into the phone.

seven

The moment Crystal saw him, she realized it was not David who had been the man in her dreams. She had dreamed not of brown eyes but of dark blue, deepening to black with the shifting of his moods, of a voice that both soothed and excited, of strong arms that had shielded her from danger and humiliation.

She quickly explained to herself that her conversation with Etta the night before, combined with the roar of an airplane engine overhead just before falling asleep, would have prompted her senses to project the image of Adam Sutherland.

"Good morning," Adam greeted her now, rising from the table where a third place had been set. A smile dispelled the austerity of his classic features, and his hair shimmered with an aura of midnight blue where the sun touched it.

"Mr. Sutherland," Crystal acknowledged breathlessly, and after allowing herself another hurried glance, her eyes came to rest on his mother, who sat patiently, listening to their exchange, watching them. "Good morning, Etta."

"Etta?" Adam questioned, and Crystal wondered if he was surprised that she was on a first-name basis with his mother. But with pleasant camaraderie, he continued, "Normally, I wouldn't intrude on your breakfast. However, I invited myself this morning for a specific reason." He lifted the lid from the breakfast tray and bent over to

70

inhale the aroma. "We have some things to discuss—"

"Before you go off on a tangent, Adam," Etta interrupted with a trace of smugness, "we must have our morning devotions. Crystal insists upon it."

He replaced the lid on the tray then leaned back in his chair, a bland expression replacing his previous look of pleasure.

Crystal eyed Etta, who was staring innocently down at her empty plate. "I don't *insist,*" Crystal objected. "It isn't true devotion or worship if anyone feels forced."

The mood of the morning had changed entirely. She mustn't allow her beliefs to become something that separated her from others. It should be a unifying force.

"Your sensitivity is showing again, Miss Janis," Adam said, leaning toward her. His hand encircled her wrist lightly. "Do it. Please. So that we might get on with more pressing matters."

Rather than create a scene, she agreed, and Adam released his grip and settled back in his chair.

Taking the small book from her pocket, Crystal turned to the appropriate day and, hoping her self-consciousness was not evident, read about little seeds being planted, nurtured, and growing into productive plants. She ended with a short prayer, including a word for Annette Phillips and her mother, and gratitude for Adam's safe return.

"Nice," Adam commented after her "Amen." "And if God doesn't send the rain, I shall irrigate."

"How interesting." Crystal could not resist a retort. "I should like to see *you* create water, Mr. Sutherland."

He acknowledged her jibe with a nod of his head. "As soon as you have the time. But I warn you, there are miles and miles of it." He set aside the lid from the tray, took his mother's plate, and followed her instructions on how to fill it.

Crystal returned the book to her pocket. How foolish of her to make such a remark to Adam Sutherland! She wasn't doing very well planting her own seeds of faith.

Suddenly, Adam's words penetrated her thoughts. "Why do I feel I've lost half my audience?"

"Oh, I'm sorry," Crystal apologized, realizing he wanted to serve her plate. "Eggs and ham, please."

"Would you prefer that we dispense with conversation until you are fully awake, Miss Janis?"

A glance at Etta Sutherland told her nothing, for Etta was cutting her ham into bite-sized pieces as if having interest in nothing else. "It's your home, Mr. Sutherland," Crystal replied as contritely as she could manage. "You may speak whenever you wish."

"Thank you," he murmured, and Crystal was almost sure the glance Etta shot him held a trace of amusement. "Now, for my news. Mother, the government has leased our land for another five years, so we can continue the irrigation experiments."

"Oh, Adam, that is good news! I'm so glad, son."

There was genuine enthusiasm in her voice, Crystal noted, realizing how much more emotion the woman must be keeping under rigid control.

Adam talked briefly about his future plans. Then his face grew pensive. "On the darker side, Mother, I've talked with the doctors about Annette Phillips's mother. I'm afraid the prognosis is unfavorable."

Etta frowned. "Is there anything we can do, Adam?"

"We'll do whatever we can to ease their burden, of course." He waited a moment before continuing. "You need to be aware that Miss Phillips may not return to us for a while."

"Which means," Etta remarked with a dour expression, "that we must think of hiring another stranger to come into this house."

"One step at a time, Mother. In the meantime, we have Miss Janis with us through the weekend. Now, we must discuss the party." He addressed Crystal. "What shall it be—a dinner party, swimming? You decide."

"A party really isn't necessary," Crystal replied. "My friends won't mind waiting a few more days before they see me."

"That was not the impression I received the night I whisked you away from David Hamilton," Adam insisted. "It's the least we can do, inconveniencing you as we have."

"A party would be nice for you, too, Adam," Etta told him. "Your social life here at Shelomoh has been rather limited these past months."

"And yours," Crystal said, including Etta.

The woman rebelled. "Now don't drag *me* into this."

"Then I couldn't possibly—"

Etta interrupted with a snort. "Adam, do you realize we've never had anyone who made demands like this? Why, it's positively blackmail, how this girl gets her way."

Crystal recognized the remarks as light bantering, as Etta continued, "Why, I wouldn't be surprised if she were to invite some doddering old man to keep me occupied while you young people play party games."

"I'm sure she knows better than that, Mother," Adam replied, coming to Crystal's defense.

Etta blotted her lips on a napkin, then pushed herself

away from the table. "You two sit here and plan whatever you like. I have a few things to attend to in my room."

She wheeled herself into the house, and Bari closed the doors behind her.

Crystal sat uncomfortably, watching Adam pour coffee into two cups.

"Now," he said, setting the pot down. "What shall it be?"

"A little cream," she said.

"Cream," he repeated diffidently. "Miss Janis, don't you *want* to see your friends?"

When she didn't answer immediately, he leaned back in his chair. "I see," he said slowly. "Perhaps you don't. But you are still willing to stay through the weekend?"

The suggestive quality in his voice caught her attention, and her eyes flew to his and found them roving thoughtfully over her hair. A faint smile settled at the corners of his lips, and she was reminded of his penchant for blonds.

Flustered, she felt a flush heating her cheeks. "Yes . . . I mean, no . . . that is—a visit would be very nice. And it might be good for your mother," she repeated herself, reaching for the cream pitcher and adding some to her coffee. "I mean, having people in the house. She must be terribly lonely, never having any company."

"I agree with you there," he said, concerned. "But believe me, everything possible has been tried with Mother."

"How incredible," Crystal retorted, finding it hard to believe such a defeatist attitude. "Then you've given up trying?"

He toyed with his cup handle. "Sometimes it's best not to build up one's hopes." He lifted his hand to prevent her rebuttal when she opened her mouth to protest. "I know you must believe like the others at the mission station. Like Dr. Kent. He talked with Mother many times about faith, hope, and the miracles God can perform."

Adam glanced toward his mother's rooms and lowered his voice. "She did entertain hope for a while. But when it didn't materialize into reality, she attempted suicide. Should she allow herself to hope again, and meet with another disappointment, I would fear for her life. Surely, under these circumstances, you wouldn't even want to try."

"I can't imagine *not* trying," Crystal said quietly.

Adam sighed. "I know. And I'm inclined to believe you might be good for Mother. However, you won't be here long enough to achieve any long-term results. Even if you were, she doesn't allow herself any personal relationships and would resist become attached to you."

Crystal nodded. "I've detected that."

"Yes," Adam said smoothly. "But against her better judgment, she seems to like you."

Crystal could reply sincerely, "And I like your mother. I sense a very fine person buried beneath all that self-incrimination."

Adam peered at her over the rim of his cup then set it down. "You seem to have an uncanny understanding of her."

Crystal felt uneasy. "Oh, I don't claim to know more than all the professionals who have attempted to work with her. I suppose it's just an understanding of basic human nature. Your mother needs love and trust, companionship, no matter how much she protests."

"And you can give her those things?" Adam asked

curiously.

He must surely think her ridiculous, and the slight flicker of amusement in his eyes indicated as much. "No," she replied. "But *you* can."

His curt reply was no more than she expected. "Miss Janis, I don't mean to be rude. You're a newcomer here, but if you can't see that my mother's best interests are uppermost in my mind, then your perception is indeed dim."

"Oh, I'm not implying that you don't love your mother. It's just—"

"Just what?" he asked impatiently.

"I think you might take a different approach. You're more like an overbearing parent than a son."

His momentary surprise was replaced by a touch of irony in his voice. "Very cute, Miss Janis. You've only been here for a few days, and already you have the solution to a problem that has existed for eight years. Not only that, but you tell me how to behave toward my own mother."

For the second time in a very few minutes, she felt the color rise to her cheeks. "Of course I don't have the answers, Mr. Sutherland. But sometimes the viewpoint of an objective outsider is valuable, however insignificant it may seem. One should not be close-minded about that. You could at least listen."

He pushed his plate back and steepled his hands. "I'm listening."

In the face of his condescending attitude, Crystal felt more foolish than ever. "Can you remember," she began, trying not to bristle, "what it's like to be a rebellious teenager?"

He pretended thoughtfulness, his drawn brows causing

a furrow at the bridge of his nose. "No, Miss Janis, I never had that experience. At sixteen, I could fly a plane, as well as drive an automobile. Since my parents gave me freedom, responsibility, and trust, there was no reason to rebel. You see," he said pointedly, "I never had those 'Thou shalt nots' to inhibit me."

It was just as Jess and Robert had said. Adam Sutherland was an admirable man in many ways, but he did not adhere to the beliefs and values by which she lived her life and upon which she would build her future. "To continue, Mr. Sutherland, your mother's actions remind me of a rebellious teenager, and yours, those of a domineering parent."

Her words apparently failed to penetrate, for he merely replied, "Perhaps we can discuss it on the way to Umtali. We have a party to plan."

She looked at her watch. "I have duties here. It's past time for your mother's exercises."

"Bari knows how to administer them. I'm sure Mother would not mind excusing you for a while."

Because the idea of spending an afternoon alone with Adam, exploring what lay in the valley below Shelomoh, was so tempting, Crystal shook her head. "I wouldn't ask. Not to prepare for a party. I don't want to take advantage."

"Very well." His manner was brusque. "Kudsai will know what we need for the evening. It will be an informal dinner party. You might inform your friends that dinner will be at seven. By the way, whom do you plan to invite?"

"Jess, of course, and Robert. David. And Dr. Kent, if that's all right."

A curious gleam remained in his eyes when she named them. "That's six of you, including Mother."

"Oh, and you, of course," Crystal added. "You do plan

to be here?"

"I am the host, Miss Janis. The party was my idea." He pushed his chair back and stood, looking down at her. "I would not, for anything in the world, miss seeing you in action."

Even Etta, while doing her exercises and amid protests to the contrary, was unable to hide her interest in the upcoming festivities.

"I've invited Dr. Kent," Crystal told her.

"My dear, he and I have absolutely nothing to say to each other. He tried harder than all the others, but I alienated him, along with everyone else. Besides, I've heard everything he has to say."

"Did he tell you about his war experiences?" Crystal asked.

Etta looked at her sharply. "What war experiences?"

Crystal merely gave her a sly look. She had no idea! Only that the novel she was reading to Etta had provoked memories she was willing to share. Etta remembered war-torn Europe and the years when her family took her to safety while Reggie faced danger every day. She had cried and prayed for him daily. At least, Crystal realized, there had been a time when prayer was important to Etta Sutherland.

"I hope you don't mind my including him."

Etta stifled a yawn. "It couldn't possibly make any difference to me. However, I'm sure he won't accept your invitation."

When Crystal called Jessica, she told her to to be sure to ask Dr. Kent to be prepared to talk to Etta about the war.

"What war?" Jess wanted to know.

"*Any* war," Crystal replied desperately. "Surely he was in *some* war."

"All I can say, Crys, love," Jess said, "this is going to be *some* party!"

Finding something to wear was another story. Crystal hadn't brought many clothes, and they all seemed either too dressy or too casual. She finally decided on a simple white dress with narrow shoulder straps. With a gold belt and high-heeled sandals, it should do nicely.

Etta insisted that Crystal take the afternoon off to get ready for the party, so after a nap, she took a leisurely bath, giving extra attention to her freshly shampooed hair. Curling it on the ends, she brushed it away from her face, exposing round gold earrings, and let it fall in soft curls that rested on her shoulders.

As time for the party neared, excitement colored her cheeks, but she added a faint blush, a trace of gray eyeshadow, mascara, and raspberry gloss on her lips.

Hearing a sound at the door, she turned quickly to see Bari's hand raised as if to knock.

"Ah," she gasped. "You are . . . beau-ti-ful! You want to know when mistress's hair shampooed?"

"Yes, thank you, Bari. I'll be right in," she said, unplugging the curling iron.

"What is that contraption?" Etta asked skeptically when Crystal entered her room, looking for an outlet to plug in the iron.

"You said no curlers in your hair," Crystal replied innocently. "But this is a miracle-worker. And it won't hurt at all."

"Why do you bother?" Etta asked with a sigh.

Crystal looked at her watch. "There's still about thirty minutes before our guests arrive, and Kudzai has an army of people preparing the tables and food. So what else is there for me to do?"

"You know this is utter foolishness," Etta complained while Crystal curled her hair. "I don't want to look like a clown."

"Is that how *I* look?" Crystal asked, wide-eyed.

"Oh my, no!" Etta exclaimed in a rush of words. "I should have said something when you entered the room. But that contraption unnerved me. My dear, you are a lovely young woman." She lowered her voice. "You don't belong here. You should be out on the town, with your young man."

"He's coming tonight," Crystal replied brightly, hoping Etta would not retreat into another of her depressive moods. There'd be no shaking her out of it. "We'll have a much better time here than 'on the town,' as you call it. You see, Etta, neither David nor I go in for exotic nightlife."

Etta sighed. "Life has such strange twists. We who would love to be out there, cannot. You who can, don't care to."

That was the closest Etta Sutherland had come to admitting that she would prefer a different kind of life from the one she was presently leading, Crystal thought to herself, but it would not be wise to point that out. "Now stop fussing, and indulge me," she said playfully, knowing better than to try a drastic change from Etta's usual appearance.

Finally Crystal turned Mrs. Sutherland to look at herself in the mirror.

Instead of a severe knot at the back of her head, Etta's white hair was arranged in a stylish upsweep, with wispy tendrils waving gently about her face. Rich creams had softened the lines of her face, and a light blush added color. A touch of green eyeshadow gave contrast to Etta's dark eyes, helping to alleviate the apprehension that had settled in them.

Overcome, Etta looked away from her reflection. "I haven't worn makeup since—"

At Bari's pained glance, Crystal surmised it had been at least two years. "We might as well go all the way then," she said, and applied a dab of peach lip gloss.

Complaining that her feet had shrunk and that none of her shoes fit anymore, Etta settled on a pair with a strap across the instep. Her peach-colored silk blouse, with a fine lace collar, completed the picture of grace and elegance.

"You're a very beautiful woman," Crystal said with sincere admiration. "You should not hide yourself away."

"Don't talk like that," Etta said harshly, then began to rummage through one of her many jewelry boxes. "These will do," she said, then added, "won't they?" Sudden dejection touched her features. "I used to be so sure of everything."

"They're just the right touch," Crystal agreed, pretending not to notice Etta's distress. She fastened the pearls, and found matching earrings.

"Why am I doing this?" Etta asked in a near whisper.

Crystal replied as honestly as she could. "Because it doesn't matter—" She paused. "Or maybe . . . because it does."

Etta lifted her chin. "We don't know which, do we?

Now, let's go downstairs and prove that I haven't forgotten how to play hostess."

eight

"Mother, are you ready?"

Adam's knock at the bedroom door sent a quiver of uncertainty through Crystal. Patting a stray hair into place, she turned Etta's chair so her son could enjoy the full effect when he entered the room.

"Come in, Adam," Etta invited.

He paused at the threshold, taking in the transformation. Then, bowing low, he touched his lips to her hand. "You're very lovely this evening, Mother."

"Thank you, Adam," Etta replied, like a queen receiving the homage due her. "Now shall we go downstairs?"

Sitting erect, Etta wheeled herself to the elevator as if her chair were Cinderella's coach on the way to the grand ball. The others followed in her wake.

When they reached the first floor, the door opened, and Adam stood aside to let Etta pass. "If you need me for anything, Mother, I'm sure you'll let me know."

"Of course, Adam," she replied and rolled swiftly toward the back of the house.

Only then did Crystal draw an easy breath. This discourse between mother and son was, no doubt, the revival of a ritual from days gone by. Adam was relinquishing some of his authority. Etta was taking advantage of it. But it was a game. And they all knew it.

When his mother, accompanied by Bari, disappeared into the kitchen to preside over the last-minute preparations for the party, Adam looked down at Crystal. She waited, expecting some word of appreciation.

"There is something—" he hesitated—"but this doesn't seem to be the time." Turning abruptly, he walked swiftly down the hallway and out into the courtyard.

Suddenly, despite the warm temperature outside, the balmy breezes so ideal for an outdoor gathering, the climate where Crystal was standing cooled perceptibly. What had prompted this strange mood in Adam? Did he feel that she had interfered? Or was he afraid that Etta would not be able to make this sudden transition brought on by her more youthful appearance? Surely he knew that it would take more than a little makeup or a new hairdo to change what lay buried inside the woman.

No, Etta Sutherland was playing a game. Crystal only hoped it was a harmless game. *I'll be here only one more day,* she reminded herself. *What can possibly go wrong in a day?*

"You're our guest tonight," Etta informed Crystal when she met her later in the courtyard. "Make yourself at home, and don't you dare attempt to give orders to anyone. Especially not to me."

Crystal laughed, noticing that Bari stood well back, discreetly unobtrusive, as she watched her daughter Lalani and several other dark-skinned women putting the final touches on the serving tables. When they finished, they looked to Etta for her approval.

Each round skirted table, centered with an arrangement of fresh flowers, had been set for four. Bowls of fruit in larger containers of ice, along with platters that would hold the barbequed quail legs and other delicacies Kudsai had prepared, adorned the serving tables. At the far end of the courtyard, Adam was overseeing the cleaning of the glass globes atop pedestals, placed at appropriate intervals and ready for night lighting.

Everything seemed to be in order, but Crystal felt a moment of apprehension. She'd much rather be involved in the activity than the guest of honor. Still, Etta was proving something tonight, so Crystal left her to her supervision and walked down along the pool, enjoying the reflection of the spectacular African sunset streaking the water with crimson and burnt umber. Perhaps she could persuade Etta to swim again. The exercise would increase her agility and stamina—

Hearing the hum of an airplane overhead, she shaded her eyes and looked up to see a small white craft with red markings. She waved, certain her friends would be looking down.

Suddenly Adam strode over in her direction. Stopping to take a coat and tie from the back of a chair, he approached, draping the tie around his neck. "You know how to tie one of these?"

"I'm afraid I haven't had much experience with that kind of thing." She shrugged, embarrassed. "Who normally ties your ties for you?"

A gleam of amusement lit his eyes. "Depends. It's much easier with a mirror. Ah, Kudsai," he called and hurried over to her. The tall woman paused, put down the tray she was carrying, and tied a perfect knot, patting it once. Before she went into the house, she slashed a furious look at Crystal across the open courtyard.

"I don't think she likes me," Crystal remarked when Adam returned.

"Don't take it personally. It goes much deeper than that."

Crystal watched Adam shrug into his coat, concentrating on the stripe in his tie. But she was still concerned about the native woman's attitude. Kudsai never smiled, except at Adam.

"Crystal?"

She lifted her gaze to his.

"I think it's time I called you by your first name," he stated as a matter of fact. "Your friends might not take kindly to my treating you like one of the hired help."

His expression softened unaccountably, and to cover her growing confusion, she jested, "Does that mean I'm fired?"

"Fired?" He took a step closer, rousing the drums in her heart. "You were hired by my mother. So I can't fire you, now can I?"

"No," she whispered. Unable to breathe, she turned away. She felt his presence close behind her and recalled the night she had stumbled and he had held her safe against him.

"Crystal," he said quietly in her ear. "There is something I haven't told you—"

The admission caught her off-guard. She turned, facing him, finding him closer still, a disturbing intensity in his gaze. He opened his mouth to speak, and she saw the rise of his chest.

"I—" he began, then turned his head toward the sound of a vehicle pulling into the side driveway. "I believe our entertainment has arrived."

Several young native men and a woman poured out of a van and began setting up their musical instruments under a canopied platform, erected for the evening, Crystal guessed.

"You didn't tell me—"

"I have a few surprises of my own," Adam replied, and left her to greet the musicians.

The band was playing when her friends arrived in Adam's Bentley, driven by George. Crystal was relieved to see that the men were wearing suits and ties, and Jessica was a knockout in a green silk dress, draped to one side and adorned with an enormous brooch. Jess had always had a way with outlandishly extravagant costume jewelry, but with her height, she could carry it off.

Seeing Crystal, she rushed forward, her long dark hair bouncing on her shoulders. Giving her a crushing hug, Jess squealed. "You look terrific, Crys!" Then she stepped back to scrutinize her friend from head to toe.

"I'll second that," said David, coming up behind her. Taking her hands in his, he looked her squarely in the eye. "I thought I must have dreamed you into existence, Crystal. But here you are, more beautiful than I remembered."

"And you're every bit the flatterer *I* remember, David."

His brown eyes caressed her. "If there were not so many eavesdroppers, I'd tell you more."

"You don't leave any doubt as to where you stand, do you, David?" Robert asked with a laugh.

"Can't afford to," David replied, a broad smile spreading across his handsome face, then turned to extend his hand to his host. "Thanks for inviting us, Adam. Apparently you're a very understanding man."

Adam gave a curt nod, then turned to Robert. "I hear

you're considering a position at the hospital in Salisbury."

"It's a possibility."

"We'd hate to lose a good man," Dr. Kent added, "but in my opinion, it's an opportunity he shouldn't pass up."

Jess and Crystal walked ahead while the men talked shop. "My Robert's going to be a very important man if he accepts that position," Jess said in a low voice. "My father has a little bit to do with it . . . not to mention the fact that Adam Sutherland is on the board." She winked knowingly.

Etta had wheeled herself to a table, where she was holding court, the lap shawl covering her feet and legs. One by one, the guests stepped over to speak with her, and she greeted Jessica, Robert, and David graciously.

"Emil," she said, as Dr. Kent bent over her hand, appraising her over the top of his glasses. "How nice of you to come."

"I will come anytime you invite me, Etta. You know that."

"Yes, well," she said formally, "perhaps you will tell me of your war experiences this time, Emil."

He seemed taken aback, and Crystal knew he had been prepared for an encounter with a bitter old woman. Instead, he had found a charming old friend. Drawing up a chair, Emil sat down at Etta's table, and they began an animated conversation.

"Ah," Adam said, as another car pulled up at the far side of the house, "our final guest has arrived. Excuse me."

To Crystal's surprise, he returned with a beautiful Eurasian woman, her dusky complexion burnished by the rays of the setting sun. High cheekbones sculpted her face, and she had brushed back her dark hair into a severe chignon that set off her fine features. Her generous mouth matched the flame red flowers in her gown, a classic sheath.

"Well, well, how's the finest psychologist in Umtali?" Dr. Kent asked. He stood and smiled, taking her hand.

"I hope you're referring to *me*, Dr. Kent." Her words, accented with the crisp British sound Crystal had come to love, were accompanied by a pleasant laugh.

"Indeed I am," he assured her, returning to his seat.

"Nice to see you again, my dear," Etta told her, and Crystal knew that the lovely woman had been here before, not necessarily in a professional capacity. She and Adam appeared to be comfortable with each other.

Like David and me, Crystal thought to herself, *only different.* Their relationship seemed established, while hers and David's was just beginning.

After Adam had introduced the woman as Oleta, Etta signaled that they should take their plates to the long serving table where a tantalizing array of native dishes was on display. By the time they had filled their plates, Jess and Robert had found a place at Etta's table. Crystal led the way to the other, where Adam was seating Oleta.

Dusk settled in, and the pool lights were turned on, their illuminated globes like so many moons orbiting the courtyard.

At dinner, David's good humor and natural friendliness kept the conversation flowing at a lively pace. He had a strong grasp of politics and seemed to know enough about the irrigation project to ask intelligent questions of Adam, while Oleta pursued a crash course in American history with Crystal.

"Those drums," Crystal said during a lull in the conversation, when their attention was again turned to the entertainment. "I've heard a sound like that at night, coming from somewhere deep in the jungle. I've been tempted to investigate."

"I wouldn't advise that," Oleta warned with a frown, then changed the subject. "In another month or two, I'm planning to attend a seminar on psychology in New York City. Have either of you been there?"

While David fielded her questions, Crystal listened to the band, the dark fingers flying with an increasing urgency. For a time she was aware of nothing but the mesmerizing quality of the throbbing drums.

Feeling Adam's eyes on her, she turned, her breath catching a little in her throat. He was staring at her, his expression shuttered by the thick dark lashes. But he seemed to be studying her, evaluating. On the other hand, she thought with a pang of embarrassment, perhaps his mind was on something else and she just happened to be in his line of vision.

Crystal lowered her eyes to her glass, lifted it to her lips, and took a sip to parch a sudden thirst. When she turned her face toward David, he gave her a quick wink. Strange how his smile, the obvious admiration in his eyes, were exactly what she needed to put her at ease. David was so . . . relaxing to be around. How wonderful, she thought, when one finds a complementary mate, the one perfect person to love, trust, build a life with. Perhaps she and David would be that for each other.

"Sorry, but I have to leave," Oleta told them right after dinner, explaining that she must prepare for a conference in Salisbury beginning on Monday.

Etta was quick to follow. "Too much excitement for one day," she said, her eyes surprisingly bright. "But, please, the rest of you stay as long as you like."

Dr. Kent stood. "Wonderful seeing you again, Etta." He looked as if he would like to say more.

"Good night, Emil," Etta said simply and wheeled herself toward the house, Crystal close behind.

At her touch, Etta looked up. "No reading tonight, young lady. Bari will put me to bed, and you must enjoy this evening with your friends."

"What a generous person you are, Etta Sutherland," Crystal said, bending over impulsively to kiss her cheek.

The older woman hesitated, then shrugged. "It takes so little to make you young people happy. Good night." With that, she wheeled into the house.

When Crystal returned to the courtyard, the native band was preparing to leave. Jess had cornered Adam at the far end of the serving table being cleared by the servants, and Dr. Kent, Robert, and David were sitting at one of the tables, deep in conversation.

At her approach, David excused himself and came toward her. "Let's walk our dinner off," he said, smiling, and reached for her hand.

They walked to the poolside, then followed the walkway between the maze of hedges. "Fill me in on what's been going on here, Crystal."

Excitement colored her voice as she related the events of the past few days.

"It sounds as if you're accomplishing what no one else could, Crys." David was openly admiring.

Crystal shook her head. "I'm afraid it's largely superficial, David. Etta Sutherland knows I'm no threat to her.

I'm only temporary, so she's literally allowed me to make some cosmetic changes, that's all. Her real problems are still intact." Then she told him about stumbling into Etta's room the night they met, omitting Adam's role in the rescue. "So I think she sees me as . . . an amusing distraction."

"And Adam Sutherland? How does he view you?" David was watching her closely.

"I'm a paid employee, David. Nothing more."

There was a moment of silence, while they sorted out their own thoughts.

"Will Adam be taking off again soon on one of his business jaunts?"

"He hasn't said. But Annette Phillips may be back on Monday. If so, I'll come back to Jess's apartment," Crystal assured him.

"And if not—" he asked, pausing meaningfully—"you will stay."

"David—" She glanced up at him to find a thoughtful expression on his face, the bright moon playing with the red-gold lights in his hair. A part of her wanted to return with him to the mission station, explore their relationship, give it a chance to grow. Yet— "I can't find it in myself to give up on Etta Sutherland. I like her, David. And I never expected to."

"Your commitment is certainly not in question," he said appreciatively. "You are a person who persists in looking beneath the surface. Apparently you won't be content with applying a Band-Aid to a mortal wound."

"That's characteristic of people in my profession, David. As in yours. We realize the value of the total person." She sighed. "I think the Sutherlands would like to see me as a ray of hope for Etta. At the same time, they're *afraid* to hope. I can't tell you how my heart goes out to that woman."

Looking toward the house, quite visible in the bright moonlight, Crystal could see the glow from Etta's bedroom windows and knew she had not yet settled for the night.

"I understand some of that fear you talked about, Crystal," David said, and she turned to give him her full attention.

"You see," he began seriously, "I was in love with a girl who refused to be a missionary's wife. I had to choose between her and what I believed to be God's calling for my life."

"I didn't know—" Crystal said, touching his arm.

He placed his hand over hers. "That was years ago. It's time to move on," he said, smiling down at her. "But that sense of loss, that fear of loving and being rejected runs deep. When I first learned you were coming to Africa, I hoped you were the girl I might spend my life with."

David paused, and she knew he was waiting for a signal from her that he had said too much. When she didn't stop him, he went on, "Along with that hope is a reluctance to believe it could be true. We all see something very special in you, Crystal. But, like Mrs. Sutherland, I'm almost afraid to hope—"

Crystal didn't try to conceal the emotion she was feeling. Her eyes were moist as she responded to his heartache. "If there's anything special, David, it's not of my doing. It could only be God, reaching out to Etta Sutherland through me."

"Is there any reason, Crystal, why you must return to the

States any time soon?"

A smile spread across her face. "No, David, there isn't. I should hear from Chicago soon, about the job I applied for. But I'm not obligated to accept it. It isn't something I feel compelled to do."

"You must have challenges in your life to feel fulfilled, Crystal?" he asked thoughtfully.

"I've never wanted to settle down to the so-called good life," she admitted. "I want to be where I can make a difference. See results. Something draws me here." She stopped talking suddenly, for he was staring at her so endearingly.

"Crystal," he said softly. Then his arms went around her, and she found herself welcoming the touch of his lips on hers, wanting him to hold her close and prove to her that he was the man she needed in her life.

"I know you're here for a reason, Crystal," he said, after reluctantly moving his lips from hers. "I hope it's for me."

Crystal could honestly say, "I hope so too, David." She did not want to consider why either of them should doubt it.

"Well, *there* you are," Jess's voice rang out as they walked back into the courtyard, David's arm draped possessively around Crystal's shoulders. "We were about to round up a posse."

"This is not the Wild West, Jess," she said, laughing.

"No, but that's the wild David Hamilton."

"You're closer to the truth than you know, Jess," David replied honestly, and everyone laughed, except Adam.

Turning to Jessica, Crystal spoke up. "We haven't had a chance to say more than a dozen words to each other all evening."

"Just like the good ol' days in Chicago," Jess said, with an airy wave of her hand. "If a guy's around, he'll do his best to monopolize your time."

"Uh, why don't you two have your talk," Dr. Kent interrupted, looking at his watch. "We should be getting back to the mission soon."

As soon as Jess and Crystal were out of earshot, Crystal hissed, "What are you trying to do, Jess, insinuating that all the guys are crazy for me?"

Jess laughed. "Never hurts to let a man know that others are interested in you, Crys."

"I don't think that would matter to David," Crystal replied. "He looks at a person's heart, not at how many males they can attract."

Jess shrugged. "Yes, I suppose you're right."

Crystal tried to ignore the smug smile on Jess's lips. "Now, tell me what you and Mr. Sutherland were talking about."

"Mr. Sutherland?" Jess shrieked, then lowered her voice when the men looked their way. "You mean, Adam? Don't tell me you're not on a first-name basis by now."

"He asked me to call him Adam, but I don't think that's wise."

Jess was clearly exasperated. "Do you know how many women would be ecstatic to do that?"

"I can imagine," Crystal replied. "But there are certain rules one must abide by when employed by a man like that. Jess, it was you who warned me about his attraction to blonds."

"Well, that's to your advantage. The first step is being attracted. And he's certainly intelligent enough to know you're not his long-lost fiancée."

"Jess," Crystal said in a near whisper. "He doesn't share the same beliefs I have. You know how important that is to me."

Jess leaned forward, her face aglow. "But he's a great humanitarian. He cares about people, and that's a start. Someone like you could witness to him, change his way of thinking."

"Well, I'm not doing too well along those lines," Crystal confessed. "And there's always the risk that someone like him could lead someone like me into his lifestyle."

"Not you, Crys. Never you."

Just then Robert stepped up. "Time to go, Jessica. George is waiting to take us back to the landing strip."

Adam had disappeared into the house by the time the Bentley pulled out. Waving goodbye, Crystal watched the retreating red taillights as the car drove away. Then her hand dropped to her side. Why did she not feel that her reason for being in Africa was moving away from her, down the long drive? What had so enchanted her that she had begun to feel like she belonged at Shelomoh? What strange African spell had come over her?

Suddenly, the courtyard lights went out. At that instant, a figure darted along the trees at the other side of the driveway. She watched for a while, trying to see who was running into the jungle, then hearing a sound near at hand, she quickly turned toward the house and found herself crashing headlong into the tall figure blocking her way.

She recognized the stripe in the tie. "Adam!" she gasped, as his hands grasped her shoulders.

She twisted to get away, but his grip tightened. With a

quick turn of her head, her hair swirled around her shoulders.

That mysterious figure in the trees came as no surprise to her. She'd seen it before. What startled her was not something to be faced out there in the jungle. It was standing much closer.

"It's only me," he said softly.

Only you, Adam, she thought ironically, as she slowly turned her face toward his and looked up.

His stormy eyes held her gaze. "Crystal," he whispered, and she felt the warmth of his breath fluttering against her cheek.

"Adam—" Before she could speak, another voice uttered his name and Crystal's eyes flew open, her body stiffening at the sound.

"Mr. Adam!" Kudsai called again. "I need you, Mr. Adam! It's important!"

nine

"When we take a step toward God, Etta, He takes several toward us."

"One cannot step without movable feet and legs," Mrs. Sutherland reminded Crystal.

"I was speaking of *spiritual* steps, Etta."

The woman's eyes met hers with cool determination. "So was I. I'm as lifeless on the inside as on the outside. Now, Bari. I'm ready for the whirlpool."

Crystal flipped off Mrs. Sutherland's television set and went to her own room, a feeling of exasperation overtaking her. She had hoped, when Etta did not object to their watching a Sunday morning church service, that it would give her the opportunity to speak of spiritual matters—something Etta desperately needed to hear. As this was Crystal's last day at Shelomoh, she had to make the attempt.

They had eaten their breakfast together while watching the televised service, broadcast in English from Salisbury, and Etta had appeared interested. However, as soon as Crystal began to make a personal application, the woman made it clear that she did not want God interfering in her life.

Crystal looked out the windows. It was such a beautiful morning, with the sun blazing brightly out of a cloudless sky. Yet an aura of gloom had permeated the house all morning. It was quiet today, for all the staff except Bari

98

had gone for the day and would not return until evening. And Adam had sent word up to his mother that he would be in his study, handling some household matters.

After returning from the whirlpool, Mrs. Sutherland withdrew further into herself, as if regretting the role she had played the previous evening. She would not discuss the party but did allow Crystal to read another chapter from the novel. Then she wanted to be alone.

Etta had a light lunch in her own suite, and Crystal stayed in hers, rather than to chance going downstairs and running into Adam.

It was shortly before naptime that Bari knocked on the door of Crystal's sitting room, where she was attempting, without much success, to write to her parents.

"Mr. Adam thought this good time for talk," Bari said. "While mistress take nap."

Crystal checked her appearance—khaki skirt and short-sleeved blue blouse—and thought it quite casual compared with her usual Sunday attire. All the curl had disappeared from her hair and she had on very little makeup, but she would have to do. She slipped out of her flats and into a pair of heels, hoping the added inches would offset Adam Sutherland's intimidating height.

Descending the curved staircase, she found him watching for her. "Hello," she called, unprepared for the instant replay of the past evening that ran through her head at the sight of him.

"This must be a very boring Sunday for you," he said, turning toward the back of the house.

Crystal fell into step beside him. "It comes with the territory," she replied, not wanting to complain. But she couldn't help adding, "It *shouldn't* be boring. I know some of the staff have gone to church in Umtali. And there are many things to do on this estate. So many possibilities for your mother, even from her wheelchair. Things the two of you could do together."

"That is hardly a valid criticism," he retorted, and Crystal realized her observation was being taken as condemnation.

She looked away from his annoyed expression and focused on the kitchen doorway as they passed. "What was Kudsai's problem last night?"

"A breaker had been tripped," he answered blandly. "It would appear there was a surge of electricity . . . or that someone deliberately flipped the switch."

"Kudsai?"

He gave an affirmative nod. Opening the door, he stepped aside for Crystal to precede him into the courtyard.

But why? She opened her mouth to ask, and promptly closed it. *Wasn't it rather obvious? Kudsai did not want Adam anywhere near me,* she reasoned

They walked beside the pool, sparkling in the brilliant sunshine, and out toward the gardens.

"What did you think of the party?" he asked.

Crystal smiled. "Perfect. Thank you for your thoughtfulness." She quickly dismissed the image of dark blue eyes meeting light as he bent toward her in the moonlight. "Etta enjoyed it, too, in spite of herself."

Adam nodded. "She hasn't looked so well, nor made such an effort, in over eight years. It would be good," he said slowly, "if we did something like that more often."

"There's no reason why you couldn't."

"Not without the guidance of a certain persistent young

woman who insists upon having her own way," he replied,
a smile touching his lips, then fading at his next words.
"From what I observed, the gathering seemed to have
worked well for you and David."

Had he observed their kiss? Color flooded her face.
"Well," she said, uncomfortably, "you're right. David and
I are . . . closer."

"That seems to worry your friend Jessica."

Crystal darted him a quizzical glance. "That's a little
hard to believe, since Jess is the one who would love to
have me marry and settle permanently in Africa."

His mocking gaze held hers. "Oh, it isn't the idea of
marriage that concerns her. It's marriage to *David.*"

"But that's absurd." What kind of game was Adam
Sutherland playing this time? "No one, including David,
is perfect, of course. But we share the same values, have
much in common—"

"You have it all wrong." Adam stopped to pluck a dead
leaf from a bed of brilliant poinsettias before walking on
into the garden. "She's afraid you'll come to find David
rather boring."

"David is anything but boring," she continued defensively, pausing under a flowering jacaranda tree. "He's
exactly the kind of man I always thought I would marry.
Besides his wonderful inner qualities, he's very attractive.
And you saw how well he relates to people, how relaxed
and natural he is. Why, at our table last night—"

"Oh, come now, Crystal, you needn't be defensive."
Adam reached up and broke off one of the lavender
blossoms above her head. "I'm only quoting Jessica."

"Well, maybe Jess finds him boring, but I don't."

He shrugged slightly. "She fears it might end up like the

situation with Stuart."

Crystal gaped at him. "She told you about Stuart?"

He twirled the blossom between his fingers. "Only enough to help me understand you," he explained in an attempt to be consoling. "And I'll admit I encouraged it. After all, we've taken you on in a very responsible position. And without checking your background. For all I know, you could be an international diamond thief, or a smuggler of priceless paintings. Surely you didn't expect me to take you at face value?"

"Right," Crystal said, unable to keep the dimples from denting her cheeks. "And I might not be a blond at all. There may be dark roots under here." She put both hands under her hair, flipping it off her shoulders.

"No," Adam replied, stepping closer. "I checked that out for myself. You're a true blond all right . . . watch it!" he warned as she took a step back, almost losing her balance.

She felt the tree at her back and pressed herself against it. There was nowhere else to go.

Crystal stood motionless, holding her breath, while Adam leaned near and tucked the blossom behind one ear, his strong fingers grazing her cheek. She was aware of a musky scent, a combination of soap and aftershave. He propped his hand on the tree above her head.

"Do you know that someone either comes or goes from the jungle late at night," she said, desperately searching for a distraction. She pointed toward the jungle. "I've seen a light moving out there."

"Late at night, you say? Then I suppose we'll have to investigate."

"Be careful." Her voice was thin and breathless.

"I assure you," he replied, "I shall proceed with the utmost caution."

She ducked under his arm and began to retrace her steps through the garden. "What was it you wanted to tell me last night?"

"It's about Annette Phillips," he replied, walking along beside her. "She's not planning to return as long as her mother needs her. The doctors say she may have a couple of months, but naturally there is hope of remission and recovery." He paused to give her a sidelong glance. "I deliberately withheld that fact from you because I wanted to give you and Mother more time together, so I could observe the results."

"A test," Crystal said.

"Yes," he admitted. "To discover if I wanted to ask you to stay as Annette Phillips's replacement."

Her heart drummed wildly. "And?"

"I knew the moment I saw the remarkable change in Mother's appearance for the party. That's what I wanted to tell you last night. By the way, how is she today?"

"Not very well, I'm afraid. She's more depressed than I've seen her."

He nodded. "That's what frightens me, Crystal. Suppose she tries something bigger than a party? What happens the next day? Will she be better off, or worse?" They paused beside the pool. "Still . . . I want you to stay."

She reprimanded herself for the sudden burst of joy that danced around inside. He had just given her a perfect reason to leave. Raising hope in his mother was extremely dangerous. Yet he wanted her to stay. "It—it's your mother's decision to make, isn't it?" she asked carefully.

Adam nodded. "That's the only way we could even

hope for success. I just wanted you to know my feelings. But please don't allow me to be a hindrance."

"Why should you be?"

"Your friend was delighted with the change you made in Mother and felt we'd want you to stay. But she reminded me of your high personal standards and warned that I mustn't try to impose my lifestyle on you, mustn't tempt you with my worldly allure, my possessions, or you'd leave—" he snapped his fingers—"just like that!"

Crystal was shaking her head. "No, Mr. Sutherland."

"Adam."

"Adam. I'm not above temptation, and I do prefer riches to poverty. But more importantly, I believe in eternal values above temporal ones. And I believe that God has a man in mind for me, one who will be everything I need. And until I find him, I won't even consider marriage."

"Why would your friend think *I* would pursue you?" he asked.

Crystal shrugged. "Because . . . I'm a blond?"

"Ah, that is a definite attraction," he admitted, "but I am not so shallow as to attempt to build a relationship with a woman based on the color of her hair. You see, I've had to do some serious thinking in the past eight years—"

A movement caught Crystal's eye. "Oh, no!" she exclaimed, seeing that Etta Sutherland and Bari were on the veranda, looking down at them. "It must be past two o'clock."

"I'm sure they can manage a few minutes without you," Adam murmured.

"They shouldn't have to. Your mother is the reason I'm here." She hurried toward the house.

Adam caught up with her easily. "Then let's find out if

you will stay, or if I should plan to return you to the mission station tonight."

When they reached the second floor veranda, they found that Mrs. Sutherland had returned to her bedroom. She was sitting in front of her windows in the wheelchair, devoid of the makeup that, the night before, had taken ten years off her age.

"I'm tired," Etta said crossly, when Crystal and Adam entered the room. "And I don't wish to be disturbed. I did not sleep during naptime."

"This won't take long, Mother."

"Then, sit," she said with resignation.

Bari, who had been changing the linens, quietly left the room and Crystal perched on the bed.

"You need to decide if you want Crystal to stay on, or if you want me to make the decision about your future," he explained, and sat in the armchair across from his mother.

Etta drew in her breath. "Annette Phillips isn't returning," she said, as if she had known already.

"Not for a while . . . if ever."

"I would prefer never, Adam," she replied. "I'm sorry for what has happened. But she and I never really communicated."

Adam nodded. "Mother, I'm beginning to realize several things I didn't know before. And I think our party last night convinced Crystal that if she stays, she need not be lonely, nor isolated from her friends."

Etta regarded Crystal dully. "Do you want to stay?"

"Yes, but—"

Her reply was interrupted by Etta's toneless question.

"For me? Or for my son?"

Crystal jumped up and moved her head from side to side as if to shake away the biting coldness of Etta's voice, the unbearable accusation in her eyes. "Please," she said helplessly, trying to think of some argument to convince Etta of her integrity. "I'm sorry," she told Adam. "It would never work if she won't trust me—" She couldn't finish but turned and started from the room.

"Mother!" The word was both a plea and a reprimand. Adam strode from the room in disgust.

"Wait, child!" Etta called after Crystal. "Come here . . . please."

Crystal took a deep breath, turned, and walked back to Mrs. Sutherland.

Etta's expression reflected her deep remorse. "You misunderstood me, Crystal. I would never condemn you, nor Adam, if you were to find pleasure in each other's company. However," she hastened, sensing Crystal's discomfort, "when I saw you and Adam talking in the courtyard, I thought you and Adam had already decided . . . that a conspiracy was taking place . . . that Adam was only pretending to let me make the decision."

Crystal blinked away the moisture forming in her eyes. "I guess we're both guilty of jumping to the wrong conclusions."

"Will you forgive me . . . and stay?"

Crystal fought to control the emotional turmoil raging inside, longing for the poise and rational thinking that were supposed to mark a nurse's demeanor. She took a deep breath. "On one condition."

Etta eyed her skeptically. "And what is that?"

"You must walk."

A long silence followed Crystal's declaration.

Finally Etta murmured, "I knew that was coming, but I didn't expect it so soon." She looked down at her hands, folded on her lap. "The doctors disagree with me. And for a long time it didn't matter. Then two years ago, I decided to try to walk—" she looked up helplessly, her eyes brimming with tears—"but I couldn't," she whispered. "Oh, Crystal, don't you see? If I try and fail again, I wouldn't want to live."

Crystal's own tears streaked her face. "Etta . . . are you living now?"

Etta's lips trembled, and she shook her head. "Leave me. I want to cry. I haven't done that in so long, and there are so many things I need to say to my pillow."

"Does this mean you want me to stay . . . here at Shelomoh?" Crystal asked, her throat aching from the effort it took to speak.

"Well," Etta replied, dabbing at her tears, "we haven't finished that novel, now have we?"

A muffled sound escaped Crystal's throat as she fell forward and rested her head in Etta's lap. "I love you," she said.

"Goodness knows why," Etta replied, uncomfortably.

Crystal nodded. "Yes. He does." She rose from her knees and slipped quietly out of the room.

Pulling the door shut behind her, Crystal leaned against it for a moment, her eyes closed. Then, feeling a presence, she opened them.

Adam was standing there. Apparently, he had been listening. She saw that his long dark lashes were wet.

"For eight years, I would have given all I had for that kind of response from Mother. Then you come—" he paused, speaking with great difficulty—"and you want nothing I have to give." Without thinking, Crystal reached up and touched the moisture on his cheek. He grasped her fingers and she felt his breath warm against the palm of her hand as he pressed his lips against it. Then he released it, went to the elevator, and stood with his back turned to her.

She understood. The afternoon had been emotionally draining for everyone. Now she could write to her parents, her friends in Chicago, and Stuart. She could tell them her stay in Africa would be extended. A most important opportunity had come her way.

ten

With Etta retiring early to catch up on her rest, Crystal chose to eat in her room. When her dinner arrived, there was a little silver box on her tray. She lifted the lid and found a sealed envelope with her name scrawled across the front. She opened it and read: "Meet me in the courtyard at ten o'clock. Wear dark clothing."

The note was unsigned, and her first impulse was to laugh, remembering that Adam had jokingly mentioned the possibility of her being an international diamond thief. Could he be serious about her meeting him?

The hands of the clock passed nine, nine-thirty, quarter of ten. Even while she dressed in black slacks, long-sleeved blouse, and tennis shoes, Crystal told herself he wouldn't be there.

Upon reaching the bottom of the stairs, she felt like turning and running back up to her room. Then a shadowy figure emerged from a darkened doorway, and she drew in her breath as a hand encircled her arm.

"How do you expect to go undetected, with your hair shining like that?" he whispered gruffly.

"I didn't think I'd need a cap in Africa," she whispered back.

"Here." He held out a dark scarf.

Crystal placed the length of fabric over her head and tied it, tucking the edges of her hair under her blouse.

"Come on," Adam said. "Let's go solve our mystery."

109

They turned down the side hallway, past the servants' quarters, and out into the carport. After crossing the drive, they stepped into the shadows, where the trees blocked the moonlight.

Adam held her hand as they raced along the edge of the jungle until they came to the path. He didn't turn on the flashlight fastened to his belt, but led her deeper into the thick foliage. It occurred to her that he knew exactly where the path lay. Perhaps this was no secret to him.

"Shouldn't you turn on the light?" she asked, when he finally stopped for breath.

"Someone might see it."

"What about snakes?"

"Possible. But not likely. We keep this area pretty well cleaned out."

They grew quiet. "You don't really think there is any mystery, do you?" she said after a moment.

"I'm sure you *thought* you saw someone," he replied, "but I doubt they mean us any harm. You can rest assured that George and several others are entirely aware the moment anyone sets foot on our property."

She gasped. "Then what are we doing here?"

He turned to look down at her, his face barely visible in the filtered moonlight piercing the dense canopy of trees. "That's a good question. I'll have to admit I wrote the note on impulse. Jessica was right. Men do strange things around you."

"Jess said that?"

"Shhh." He covered her lips with one finger. "We must be quiet if we're to catch whoever it is." The finger moved over her lips. Suddenly his hand cupped her cheek.

She heard no approaching footsteps, only the sound of

distant drums throbbed upon the night air, fragrant with
the aroma of blossoms and earth.

She said the only thing that came to mind. "Is . . . is this
another of your tests, Adam?"

"I hadn't intended it to be," he said, his face very close
to hers. "But, yes, it is a test . . . for me. And I think I am
about to fail it."

"No, Adam," she had to say, but she did not sound
convincing.

"Yes," he breathed against her cheek.

Just then a scream split the night air, someone came
bursting through the trees, and a light was flashed in their
faces.

"Oh, I so sorry," came a nervous voice. "You frighten
me."

It was Lalani, a young native man close behind her.

From the house, someone triggered the floodlights, and
they began to come on everywhere, illuminating most of
the wooded area as well as the house, courtyard, and
gardens. Dogs barked frantically.

"See what I mean about being well protected?" Adam
asked Crystal in exasperation. "Go back to the house, both
of you," he ordered the two young people. "I'll handle
this."

By that time, George, in his pajamas and carrying a rifle,
had reached them.

"Everything's fine!" Adam shouted to him.

"I do you favor, Mr. Sutherland," the young man said.
"I run tell the others it false alarm." He looked from
Crystal to Adam, the gesture seeming to indicate he would
keep *their* secret if they would keep *his*.

Lalani and her friend ran lightly along the edge of the

trees, and Crystal followed, suddenly feeling like the guilty party herself. When the young man reached the gardens, he held his hands high. "Everything all right!" he yelled. "Turn out lights."

Immediately the huge floodlights were extinguished, but not before Crystal noticed several cottages she hadn't been aware of before. Looking back, she saw Adam and George just reaching the courtyard, where they could be seen by anyone eager to apprehend them.

Lalani and Crystal entered the house through the carport, to be met by a coolly indignant Kudsai. She watched without speaking as Lalani scurried into her own room and closed the door. Then turning a disgusted look on Crystal, she thrust forth her hand. "Scarf mine."

"Oh, I—I'm sorry," Crystal stammered and pulled the offending garment from her head. "I didn't know it belonged to you. Th—thank you."

Crystal raced to the second floor and stood in the alcove for a moment. Bari was fussing with Mrs. Sutherland's bedcovers. "She fine. I tell her someone set off emergency light . . . by mistake." She gave Crystal a searching look, but said nothing more and turned back into Etta's room.

Oh, no! What must the woman be thinking? Did they suspect a rendezvous between her and Adam? After all, in spite of his reputation, she had spouted *her* morals all over the place! What kind of influence could Crystal possibly have with these people if they believed she was out cavorting in the jungle with Adam Sutherland?

A week later, early on Saturday morning, George drove Crystal to the airstrip, where she met David, who flew her to the mission station.

On the way, David was full of plans for the weekend. But when they arrived, Crystal insisted upon going straight to Jess's apartment. The two friends sat at the kitchen table, lingering over coffee.

"Tell me all about Adam Sutherland!" insisted Jessica, almost before Crystal could catch her breath.

"Really, Jess," Crystal said, casting a disdainful eye at her friend, "I don't think Adam and I would even think about each other if you hadn't planted those seeds in our minds. You tell *him* how intriguing *I* am, and tell *me* how irresistible *he* is. "

"Well, Crys," Jess replied, her eyes flashing, "I'm just trying to prepare you for the danger that exists when two such personalities collide. I mean, it could be worse than a streak of lightning encountering a tree during a thunderstorm!"

"Oh, speaking of trees—" Crystal began and related the jungle incident to Jess, when all the lights had come on.

"That's just the point I'm trying to make," Jess pointed out when she had stopped laughing. "You know the story of Paul on the road to Damascus, how the bright light blinded him after he had been persecuting the Christians? Well, what do you think will happen to poor Adam if he decides to pursue you seriously?"

"He knows, as well as I," Crystal said, ignoring the regret evident in her voice, "that would be improper and ill advised."

"Was that before or after your little hunting expedition?"

"Oh, Jess, that was a mistake!" she moaned, not allowing herself to consider what might have happened if Lalani had not stumbled upon them at that precise moment. "And

114 Drums of Shelamah

we're more careful than ever now to keep our relationship strictly business—" She paused, thinking of the consequences of that fateful night. "But Kudsai is like an iceberg, and even Lalani and Bari aren't quite as open with me. My reputation is probably ruined."

"Don't let it get you down, Crys. What you're doing for Etta Sutherland compensates for all the rest."

"I hope so, Jess. But sometimes, one wrong action can undo all the good a person has done."

"Well, you're not to worry this weekend. Just enjoy every minute of the fabulous time we've planned for you!"

The weekend was a whirlwind of activity. At the Wanki Game Reserve, while riding in the Land Rover, they saw an amazing variety of animals—from elephants to purple-breasted bee eaters! Crystal summed up the animal spectacular in a single phrase, "A zoo with no cages!"

They stopped once and climbed up onto an observation deck, gazing out in awe upon zebras, elephants, giraffes, antelopes, and large colorful birds. Crystal was fascinated. "This is like being on safari!"

"The animals can run wild," said David, "yet they're protected."

Protected, Crystal thought, looking at the landscape of dun-colored grasses and undulating hills. *Protected.* That's how she felt with David, looking up to find a twinkle in his warm brown eyes.

In Salisbury, they shopped for some good walking shoes for Etta, "just in case," and dined in one of the finer restaurants.

While they were having dessert, Crystal brought them

up to date on the woman's progress. "She's been in the
water several times already. Just short sessions at first, but
long enough for her legs to grow accustomed to her weight.
And when she begins to tire, she swims for a few minutes."

"How do you manage?" David asked quickly.

"Bari helps. And Adam, too, sometimes." She felt,
rather than saw Jess's significant look when she used her
employer's first name, and David concentrated on his
raspberry trifle.

"So," Crystal continued, her words tumbling over them-
selves, "for the first time in many years, she really does
need to rest on the weekends. I've already consulted with
her doctor over the phone, and I plan to talk to a psychologist while I'm here. By the way, I'm also open to any
advice you too may have to give."

As the evening wore on, Crystal became aware that
David had been unusually quiet. That could easily be
explained, however, she reminded herself. A teacher
wouldn't have as much to contribute to a conversation
about Etta Sutherland as Robert, the surgeon, and Jess, the
nurse.

On the long drive back to Sanyati, Crystal leaned back
comfortably, and David put his arm around her. In the
front seat, Robert and Jess kept their own conversation
going, accompanied by a music tape, turned low.

"I'm beginning to wonder," David said close to her ear,
"if your purpose in Africa is Etta Sutherland, and not me
at all."

She turned in the seat to regard him with surprise. There
was no sign of jealousy, only a trace of regret. "Couldn't
it be both?"

"That's what I'm hoping, Crystal. You're everything,

and more, that any man could want." His eyes were searching as they gazed into hers. "*Any* man."

He drew her to him and brushed her lips with his. "Nothing has changed between us, has it, Crystal?"

"No, David," she could say truthfully. "Nothing has changed."

Early Sunday morning, Crystal awoke with a stiffness in her muscles. Clad in a short cotton nightgown, she entered the kitchen where she'd heard Jess rummaging around. "Do you realize," she said, stretching out the kinks in her back, "that I could become spoiled, living up there at the Sutherlands?"

"Better beds than mine, huh?" Jess opened the refrigerator and took out a carton of eggs.

"Immeasurably. Not only do I sleep on a cloud, but my meals are sent up on a dumbwaiter and served to me from silver trays. Besides that, I don't even have to make my bed."

"Think of it," Jess clucked. "All that, and heaven, too! Not to mention a nice fat paycheck!"

"I objected, Jess," Crystal said. "But they wouldn't listen. And I can honestly say, none of that can even begin to compare with the satisfaction of seeing the changes in Etta Sutherland."

"I know that, Crys. It looks like you might be in Africa for a long time."

"As long as she needs me, and wants me here," Crystal said, moving over to the window to watch a small red and black bird pecking at the dry ground.

"Which just might be permanently," Jess replied, cracking the eggs into a bowl. To break the serious mood, she called out, "I'm not your personal maid, so get over here and help me. And just wait till you see where we're going to church this morning!"

Crystal would never have guessed! The "church" service at the "bore hole," a primitive-looking well surrounded by a square brick wall about two feet high and six feet long, was another unforgettable experience. They had arrived in the bush, after driving for miles down dusty paths no wider than the Land Rover.

"The government drills these holes, sometimes at one-mile intervals," Jess explained, "depending upon the closeness of the villages. The people come here for water, sometimes twice a day."

"Which makes it a perfect place for a church service," Crystal said, understanding.

She watched as two women in bright dresses, red scarves wound around their heads, pumped water into a barrellike container, while a couple of little boys in short pants chased each other around the well.

"They've come to expect someone from the mission on Sunday morning," Jess explained.

David and a young African doctor named Carl began strumming guitars, leading in the singing of some choruses, while the people gathered from all directions, some spilling out of the round thatch-roofed krawls set back among the trees. A few men strolled in to take their seats on the hard-packed dirt, but the greatest number of worshipers was women, carrying barrels on their heads or babies on their backs.

After the singing, David talked about God, his simple message translated into Shona by Carl. In the middle of the service, while David was explaining the plan of salvation, two cows ambled over to lap the water trickling from the pump.

"Welcome, Bossy," David said with a grin. When Carl interpreted, there was a ripple of amusement through the crowd.

Suddenly Crystal felt a tug on her hair. She turned quickly and saw a little round-eyed boy, who jerked his hand back guiltily. When his lower lip quivered, Crystal smiled reassuringly, and the adults looking on nodded in approval.

"I hope I wasn't too much of a distraction," Crystal said on their way back to Sanyati.

"Haven't been so distracted in years," David replied smoothly.

She gave him a sidelong glance. "I'm talking about at the bore hole."

"Nah," he assured her. "No more of a distraction than the cows."

"Well, you asked for that one!" Jess whooped.

After lunch in the hospital cafeteria, David gave Crystal a tour of the school where he taught the high-school-age students. It was not an elaborate structure, but adequate.

"The students take their studies seriously," he said. "Sometimes a family can afford to send only one of their children to school. And sometimes payment is in the form of a chicken, or vegetables from their garden."

"What wonderful work you're doing, David." Crystal was more impressed than ever with the man's sense of mission and dedication.

"We can do something here, Crystal, that can't be done

in American schools. We can read from the Bible." David frowned.

"Sometimes I wonder if I'm needed more in America, than in Africa."

"Are you serious, David?"

He paced near his desk, his hands deep in his pockets. "I've been thinking about it a lot. I'd like to have a little church somewhere. Perhaps a small mission church in America. A wife. Two little girls and a boy—" Looking over at Crystal, he tried to read her expression. "How does that sound to you?"

There was no doubt about it. David Hamilton was one of the finest human beings Crystal had ever met. She'd be crazy to think otherwise. "It sounds . . . perfect," she admitted with a tightening of her throat.

She turned and ran her finger across a desktop. Surely, if she and David were meant for each other, he wouldn't be whisked away to America, not if her place was at Shelomoh, with Etta Sutherland.

It was Adam, not George, who met the plane when David returned Crystal to the airstrip later that evening. David kissed her goodbye reluctantly, promising to fly over to take her to dinner in Umtali sometime during the week.

Adam was quick to relieve her of her packages and handed her into the passenger seat with an unusually gentle touch. "Mother missed you . . . and so did I."

Crystal closed her eyes as Adam maneuvered the sleek silver car around the curved roads. It was good to be back. Really good.

Her first stop, after reaching the house, was Etta

Sutherland's bedroom.

"Don't you knock anymore?" The irascible voice belied the brightness in Etta's eyes when she spotted Crystal.

"I just couldn't wait to show you what I brought you." She sat on Etta's bed and handed her the first box.

Crystal hadn't expected anything more than tolerant acceptance of the walking shoes. But when she opened the box containing the silver slippers, Etta's face glowed. "How lovely!" she exclaimed with genuine delight, turning the shoes this way and that to admire them from all angles.

"They're a half size smaller than your others. So they should fit."

"Let's find out," Etta said and pulled the light covering up to expose her feet. After Crystal slipped them on, she added, "Comfortable, too." She looked into Crystal's expectant face. "I'll repay you for them, of course."

"Of course," Crystal replied. "But not with money." She removed the shoes, recovered Etta's feet, and set the boxes aside. "Now to get back to our book."

Before she could begin to read, Bari walked in with a silver tray, containing a bowl of chips, two champagne glasses filled with ice, and a large bottle of Coke.

The card on the tray read: "An American prescription to ease the pain of leaving your friends. Welcome home, Adam."

"Don't worry, Etta," Crystal said, feeling her face grow warm. "If the Coke keeps us awake, we can sleep late in the morning."

eleven

"From Gwen," Mrs. Sutherland said, eyeing with suspicion the envelope that had come with Monday morning's breakfast. "Wonder what she has to say."

Crystal took a bite of her omelet. Etta read the letter while her eyes betrayed everything from wistfulness to resignation. "Gwen is coming for her annual visit. Without Trent and the children." She replaced the letter in the envelope, laid it on the table, and shoved it aside. "They're all so busy, you know."

"When is she coming?" Crystal asked, recognizing the bitter note in Etta's voice as a cover-up for her inner hurt.

"Soon." Etta poked at the omelet on her plate. "That's all she said. She'll fly in to Salisbury, and if Adam is not around, she'll rent a commuter plane to bring her here. Then what will she do?"

Crystal shrugged lightly. She knew it wasn't wise to become too involved in another person's family matters.

Etta proceeded to answer her own question. "She will kiss my cheek, then get in touch with Oleta, and they'll go into Salisbury and buy out the shops. Always the same."

"Oleta?" Crystal dared to question.

Etta swallowed her bite of food. "They're best of friends," she explained, then took a sip of orange juice. "Grew up together. Went to college together in London. Quite often Oleta will stay at Gwen's while her husband conducts business in London."

"Whose husband?" Crystal asked.

"Oleta's."

"Then she's married?"

Etta selected a hot blueberry muffin and buttered it. "Oh," she said, before taking a bite, "you're wondering why Adam would have invited a married woman to your party."

Crystal shrugged. "It's really none of my business."

"Well, I must say *I* was surprised. You see, Oleta and Gwen are several years older than Adam. He has tolerated their insufferable behavior since early childhood. And those girls could be cruel, especially during the teen years." She touched her napkin to her lips. "But it wasn't until I got to thinking about it that I realized why he invited her."

"Because he didn't want to be the odd person at a party?" Crystal guessed, reaching for one of the aromatic muffins.

"Exactly," Etta agreed. "The availability of lady-friends in Umtali is limited, and he discovered Oleta's husband was out of town on business, so she was the ideal prospect for his little dilemma. Or maybe," she added, just when Crystal thought the subject was closed, "he wants to make friends with her now that they're both adults. 'Bury the hatchet,' as you Americans would say."

Crystal swallowed her bite of muffin, and continued the charade. "Or maybe he needed her professional services."

Etta arched an eyebrow at the insinuation. "There could be many reasons," she granted, "such as, wanting us to think he's involved with someone, which he isn't. Oh, not that he doesn't have women friends, but there's been no one special. Not since Elise." She shook her head. "I never thought they were right for each other."

Crystal poured coffee for them both, and tried to look disinterested.

Etta, in a rare talkative mood, kept up her running monologue. "But when does a man listen to his mother?" she asked. "When the bells are ringing, who can hear anything else?"

"The bells?" Crystal questioned with a chuckle.

"Oh, you know what I mean. That must be the way you feel about that young man of yours. David?"

Crystal smiled. "David Hamilton. He's a very fine man. But love is a lot more than hearing bells ring."

"But—" Etta gave Crystal a knowing look—"is it really love without it?" She turned her gaze to the view from her window, remembering. "I never did use that phrase with Reggie. Not after we came to Africa. I would tell him I heard drums beating when he looked at me. Oh, I'm boring you," Etta apologized. "You have that faraway look in your eye."

"I was thinking about the drums."

"Drums?" Etta questioned immediately. "What drums?"

Strange, that Etta didn't know about the drums. Perhaps with age, her hearing had become impaired. "From the jungle," she said, pointing toward the mountains rising into the sky. "Every night, there's the sound of throbbing drums."

"Oh, my dear," Etta said, laying her hand on Crystal's in a gesture of uncharacteristic intimacy, "that could mean only one of two things."

"Please go on."

Etta took a deep breath, as if she were about to impart some dark secret. Even her voice took on a mysterious quality. "There's a saying about this continent, that Africa has a heartbeat. And when a person hears the drums, it is either love . . . or voodoo."

Crystal laughed uneasily, not sure she was enjoying Etta's little game. "It must be true then," she said off-handedly, "since I've experienced both. Voodoo, in my dream. And love, with David Hamilton."

There was a long pause. "Do you really love this David?"

Crystal collected her thoughts as she washed down her muffin with a sip of orange juice. "I think," she said with complete candor, "that it would be impossible *not* to love David."

Looking at her watch, Crystal quickly rose from her chair. "Afer all our carefully made plans, we're ten minutes off schedule. The weekend has spoiled us both."

The next few days passed quickly, the hours so full that there was not time to attend to everything. Crystal and Adam had several long phone conversations with Etta's former physical therapist and physicians, and she agreed to schedule appointments for each to come to the estate for examinations and consultations.

On Tuesday afternoon, after Adam flew off to to visit some of his irrigation projects, Crystal drove Etta down to Umtali. It was a lovely little city of about 40,000, ringed with spectacular views of the mountains—the Inyangas, the Manicas, and the Vumbas.

Etta would not leave the Bentley, saying, "Everybody will stare." But when Crystal returned from making her purchases, the woman admitted she had enjoyed watching the people, many of whom were tourists, taking in the scenic wonders of the Inyanga National Park and the

Bantu ruins.

As Crystal drove through the streets, Etta spoke of the changes that had taken place during the years. Much of Umtali's industry was directly related to the Sutherlands' vast land holdings, Crystal learned.

"During those early days after Reggie's death, Adam would stand on the veranda during the dry season, looking over the parched land that spread out as far as the eye could see," Etta reminisced. "Reggie always loved the land, even when it was bone dry and brown. Adam would stare and stare, and I was afraid he'd lost touch with reality so soon after his father died and Elise left. But now I know he was making plans," she said proudly. "One evening he announced that he wanted to experiment with the land, wanted to learn all about irrigation, turn the parched land into productive soil."

Now, that productive soil was the livelihood of thousands, Crystal realized, as Etta talked on. Many of the people worked the land, producing tobacco, tea, grain, citrus fruits, and timber, much of which was processed in Umtali, then shipped into other areas on the Salisbury-Beira Railroad.

For the remainder of the afternoon, after they returned to Shelomoh, the two women leafed through fashion magazines, tried out new makeup, and examined Etta's wardrobe with plans to refurbish. They were ready for Adam's comments when he came to Etta's sitting room for dinner.

"You look younger and prettier every time I see you, Mother," Adam said, obviously delighted with the improvement he saw in her.

Etta's excitement over the afternoon excursion was still

evident during dinner. Adam added to the history lesson, explaining that Rhodesia's first teacher-training school was located in Umtali. He spoke of its parks, its gardens, its sports centers, and the Courtauld Theatre.

It was after they decided to have their dessert on the veranda, while the sun set, that silver lights danced in Adam's dark blue eyes. "How about an outing to Victoria Falls, Crystal? You'd love it."

Crystal's cheeks dimpled. "David said there is always a rainbow at Victoria Falls."

Adam's face clouded. "I had hoped to point that out to you myself. I suppose you and David already have plans to go there."

"Nothing definite," she said, disturbed by the quick change in his mood. "But it's a wonderful idea. And it would be so good for your mother."

"Oh, I couldn't possibly," Etta replied staunchly. "I'd be in the way."

"Why, Etta, you're the reason for the trip," Crystal insisted. "I doubt if Adam would have thought of it—" Realizing how she must sound, Crystal's voice trailed away, like the sun over the mountainous horizon.

"It's been a long day," Etta said, wheeling herself toward her room. "I'm going to get ready for bed. You can let me know tomorrow what sights you plan for us to see."

When Etta was gone, Crystal joined Adam at the railing of the veranda, watching the last rays of the setting sun fire the landscape. "Your suggestion was a very good one," she said, a note of contrition in her voice. "I know you're making an effort with your mother."

"Very well," he said shortly, staring at the distant mountain. "If it's all right with you, with my mother, and with David Hamilton, we'll take in some of the sights, beginning tomorrow afternoon."

"Victoria Falls is not the tallest, but it is the largest waterfall in the world," Adam explained the next afternoon as he circled above the Zambezi River where the spectacular falls fell into the gorges, creating a magnificent rainbow.

Etta sighed. "Reggie and I came here often."

"Look." Adam pointed. "The spray creates its own special rain forest . . . even in the dry season."

"Africans call it 'Mosiotunya'—" began Etta.

"Which means 'the smoke that thunders,'" Adam finished.

The following day they traveled, again by plane, to the great ruins of Zimbabwe. Massive stone walls, built of granite, rose thirty feet into the air, with a conical tower slightly higher.

"It may have been a lookout tower, or perhaps a place of worship," Adam explained. "When the Africans take over the rule of Rhodesia," he went on, as if convinced it would happen, "then the name will be changed to Zimbabwe, in honor of the ancient kingdom located here."

"Gold and copper objects have been found here," Etta added, "and all sorts of narrow passageways are open for exploration. You may be interested to know, Crystal, that the Zimbabwe ruins are thought to be the palace of the Queen of Sheba, or even a temple of King Solomon."

Crystal stored away these treasures, to be relished long after she returned to the States.

During the next few days, Adam had to spend time at his

irrigation spots, since the dry season was now upon them. He was usually back by nightfall, however. Crystal insisted upon their dressing for dinner each evening, knowing that Adam's attentions to his mother, although she often fluffed off his compliments, were a vital step in her growing acceptance of herself as a lovely woman of worth and value, with every reason to live.

Though they had not yet progressed to the main dining room, this time of sharing their activities, feelings, and thoughts had, the week before, become the most important part of their day. Sometimes, when Adam did not have a late appointment or reports to file, their conversation extended beyond dinner, and the three of them lounged on chairs in the courtyard.

Although quite cooperative, and even pleased with her accomplishments in the pool, Etta was not ready to try what she described as "contraptions" that might enable her to walk on a hard surface.

Since Etta was making such remarkable progress, Crystal decided to abide by two new rules. First, she made a point not to speak privately with Adam, lest Etta revert to any suspicion that they were making plans without her knowledge.

The second she shared with David when he called on Friday morning to learn whether she planned to return to the mission station for the weekend. "Not now, David. Maybe next weekend." She explained that dinnertime had become so special for Etta, she didn't want to break the pattern that had just been established. "Preparing her mind to accept the possibility of walking is far more difficult than preparing her body."

David accepted her decision without question. "Then

I'll see you next weekend," he said wistfully. "Let's plan to see Victoria Falls and the Zimbabwe ruins."

"I'd love to," she replied, and meant it. She'd seen the scenic wonders with her head in the clouds, so to speak. It would be wise to see them with her feet planted solidly on the ground.

It was early the following week that everything changed. A plane rumbled overhead just as Etta and Crystal were finishing breakfast. "That has to be Gwen," Etta said irritably, glancing up at the small commuter plane circling for a landing. "She said she'd call first." Self-consciously, Etta smoothed her hair. "We'd better go downstairs."

When Mrs. Sutherland rolled into the kitchen to see Kudsai about the dinner menu, Adam led Crystal out into the courtyard. "I haven't had a chance to tell you," he said, "and who knows when the opportunity will come again, with Gwen here."

"Tell me what?" she asked, almost fearfully.

"This past week or so has been more fulfilling for me and my mother than any during the past eight years. My gratitude extends beyond words."

"I can't take all the credit," Crystal reminded him. "It was time for someone to urge her. I think she simply wasn't ready before."

"Perhaps," he said. "But the fact remains that it was you who accomplished it. I wouldn't be surprised if we all have dinner in the main dining room this evening— Mother, Gwen, myself, and," he added warmly, "you."

"Oh, this is a family time," Crystal objected. "Really, I don't mind eating in my room. I wouldn't want to intrude."

"Intrude?" He gave a short little laugh. "*Invade* might be a more appropriate word. You have so invaded our lives that we wouldn't be able to function without you at the table, talking about your wonderful ideas for my mother, seeing her response. I want Gwen to see the two of you in action."

With his eyes on her, she was suddenly conscious of her appearance—hair brushed back from her face and twisted into a knot, no makeup, a ridiculous army-green jumpsuit thrown on over the swimsuit she would be wearing for Etta's water therapy in the pool. It would be afternoon before she'd have time to make herself presentable for dinner.

No, the admiration she saw in his eyes surely had nothing to do with the way she looked at this moment!

The feel of Adam's hand on her shoulder put an end to her thoughts. Putting his finger over her lips, he pointed to one of the jacaranda trees on which a strange-looking creature was perched on a limb.

"Chameleon vulgaris," Adam whispered, leaning close to her ear. "Just don't make any sudden movements, and he won't."

"You mean he might attack us?"

"I mean he might run away." Adam gave a throaty chuckle.

"He looks like a prehistoric animal," Crystal whispered.

"See that eye looking at us? He has one on the other side that looks in the opposite direction at the same time." When she gave him a skeptical look, he went on. "It's true. That's how he compensates for not being able to move his head." Drinking in her presence, he added, "And at the moment, neither can I."

When she tried to protest, he turned her face toward him. "I must say this. You have brought life into this household, into my mother's life, and into my own. You're a miracle worker."

"Oh, no! Only God can work miracles."

"But He uses people, doesn't He?" he countered.

A sudden movement caught her eye, and she stepped away just as Etta wheeled out into the courtyard. The chameleon darted around on the other side of the tree.

"I don't want you to feel that Gwen's presence will diminish our need—" His gaze moved beyond her, and he added distantly—"of . . . you—"

The last word was spoken in a whisper, barely distinguishable. But she could read his expression. His face paled, his lips parted in surprise, and the look in his eyes was one of total disbelief.

Crystal turned her head in the direction of his gaze. A generously proportioned woman, with short dark hair, had reached Etta and was kissing her on the cheek. But it was the figure standing a few feet from Gwen that had halted Adam's speech in midsentence.

Without being told, Crystal knew that the tall blond had stepped out of the past. Adam's past. And her eyes were for him alone.

twelve

With a light touch of his hand at the small of Crystal's back, Adam guided her toward the trio across the courtyard. He moved slowly and deliberately.

Seeing her brother, Gwen turned her face for his kiss. But Crystal knew he was staring at the blond again, as if he couldn't believe his eyes. The sun, striking her hair, turned it to golden waves, framing her lovely face like a halo.

"Adam, I hope you don't mind my barging in like this," she said in a throaty voice, uncertainty reflected in her green eyes. "It seemed like a good idea when Gwen mentioned it."

Adam's eyes moved to his sister.

"Elise and I ran into each other at one of those insufferable obligatory dinner parties, Adam," she explained. "When I learned what she was going through, I thought Africa would be the perfect place for her to get away for a while."

"It did sound perfect, Adam," Elise said softly. "You were always so good at . . . helping me with my little problems."

"She and Judson are—" Gwen began, glancing at Elise.

"Our marriage has become unbearable, so we've decided to separate," Elise continued. Her eyes darted away, searching for some distant object on which to focus. They landed on Crystal, leaning against the edge of a table near

132

Etta's wheelchair. Slight curiosity registered on her face, but she went on with her explanation, drawing a deep breath. "We'll probably . . . get a divorce."

"Like I told Elise," Gwen put in, easing the awkward moment, "there's plenty of room here."

Adam agreed with enthusiasm. "Of course! She can stay in the room next to yours and above—" He looked at Crystal, as if suddenly remembering her presence. "Elise, Gwen, I'd like for you to meet Crystal Janis."

Crystal ignored Adam's outstretched hand. She was quite close enough for her "How do you do?" to be heard, without walking the few feet to join him.

Each of the women murmured a polite greeting. When nothing else was volunteered, Gwen filled the gap of silence. "Friend of yours, Adam?"

"No, no," he answered quickly, too quickly, Crystal thought. "At least, not in the way you undoubtedly mean, sis. We're very careful about our remarks, though. We say the wrong thing, and poof!" He gestured, circling with his hands. "Like a puff of smoke, she'll be gone. See? She's already turned her face away from us."

At Adam's remark, Crystal again faced the group, wishing the earth would swallow her. She felt like such a ninny in front of these beautiful women, so fashionably dressed, while she stood in her green safari costume and lost her nerve.

"Crystal has changed our lives completely," Adam said, on a serious note. "Mother and I would like her to stay with us forever."

"Forever, Adam?" Gwen questioned, with a lift of her brow.

"Permanently," he corrected. Amusement curved his

lips at Gwen's confused expression. Then he held out his hand toward Elise. "If we're to solve your problems, perhaps we should get started."

Her face lit up with her smile, and her green eyes narrowed dreamily as she moved toward Adam. They began to stroll down the walkway toward the gardens.

Crystal pulled out a chair and sat down, while Gwen came over to join her, and Etta wheeled herself closer.

"Wonderful to be here," Gwen said, inhaling the fresh morning air. "Now tell me what's been happening with you, Mother."

Feeling much like a chameleon who could not move its head, Crystal felt as if one of her eyes was trained on Etta and Gwen, while the other observed Adam and Elise. The couple had paused along the path, and Elise lifted a hand to touch Adam's face—

"Crystal," Etta said, reaching over to pat her hand, "this is the second time I've spoken to you."

"Oh, I'm sorry," she apologized. "I guess my mind was elsewhere."

"I was just telling Gwen that you've been like a daughter to me."

Crystal knew Etta meant the remark as an expression of acceptance, and perhaps as an invitation for Gwen to express her own love and concern.

But when Gwen replied, "That's wonderful, Mother," Crystal detected the restraint in her voice, as if Etta had accused her of failing to live up to her responsibilities. That remark alone could alienate Gwen before any kind of friendship could begin between them.

"I know I should visit more often, Mother," Gwen said. "But it—it's difficult."

"Yes, I know you're busy, Gwen," Etta replied with a sense of resignation. "Too busy."

"Oh, Mother." Gwen stood and stared helplessly down at Etta. "This is one of the reasons I don't visit more often. You're so accusatory. And—and argumentive. It makes me uncomfortable."

"You're uncomfortable?" Etta scoffed, looking up into her daughter's face. Then she shook her head and turned her wheelchair toward the house. "I'd like to get my exercises out of the way," she tossed over her shoulder. "After I've dressed, Gwen, I'll come down and we can discuss the children."

"All right, Mother." Tension showed on Gwen's face, deepening the lines around her eyes, and several gray hairs were noticeable in her thick dark hair. Crystal suspected she'd not had an easy time of it.

"It's always the same," Etta complained on the way upstairs. "Gwen doesn't want to be here."

"But she loves you very much," Crystal countered.

With a wave of her hand, Etta dismissed the comment. "And I *don't* want to get into the pool this morning."

With Etta in this mood, Crystal knew it would be a waste of time. "It's all right to miss occasionally."

"And another thing," Etta demanded petulantly, "I don't want you discussing me with Gwen."

"She would be pleased to know what we're doing," Crystal suggested, but Etta was adamant.

"Go ahead and get dressed," Etta said after her exercises. "And take your time. Gwen and I will be somewhere around the house . . . if she stays that long."

Crystal took Etta at her word, so she bathed leisurely and

shampooed her hair with special care. She took extra pains with her makeup and chose a blue dress with a full skirt that she knew was flattering to her trim figure. Then, fastening pearl earrings in her earlobes and stepping into her high-heeled sandals, Crystal took one last look at her reflection and went in search of Etta.

Hearing noises across the hall, she knew that Bari and Lalani were busily making preparations for the unexpected guest—dusting, putting out fresh linens, opening windows in the two bedrooms.

In the hallway, she encountered Bari. "Mistress in Mr. Adam's study," she said. "Want to look over household checkbook, she say." Bari rolled her eyes toward the ceiling. "First time in many year."

"Should I . . . disturb her?" Crystal wanted to know.

"Yes, please," Bari returned, and a worried look came into her eyes. She sighed and carried an armload of towels into one of the bedrooms.

Crystal hadn't been to Adam's study before, although she knew it was located next to the drawing room at the front of the house. She descended the staircase and turned to her left. The door was open.

At her knock, Etta glanced up. "I was just coming out," she said and closed the ledger in front of her. She moved away from the heavy wooden desk.

On the left was a comfortable-looking dark leather couch and two matching chairs, with an antique table between. Against the outside wall a fireplace rose to the ceiling. It was an inviting room, decidedly masculine.

"Let's go into the courtyard," Etta said, not bothering to explain why she suddenly had the urge to check records. Maybe she had decided to take an even greater interest in household affairs again, Crystal told herself.

Etta had done her own makeup, and Bari had learned to arrange her hair, so the older woman looked quite attractive today. But there was a look of strain on her face.

"Where is everybody?" Crystal asked when they were outside.

"Let's sit here, on the lounge chairs," Etta said. "Then we'll chat."

After they were settled, Etta explained that Adam, Elise, and Gwen had gone into Umtali. "Gwen will have lunch with Oleta. They said they know I need my afternoon nap, so they won't be back until time for dinner."

"That's . . . thoughtful."

"Thoughtful!" Etta sneered. "They're probably discussing what to do with me right now!"

"Do with you? What do you mean?"

"Oh, Gwen claims she can't bear to see me in a wheelchair. And the children feel the same way. But you know what they really mean?"

Crystal shook her head, waiting for the rest.

"It means they don't want me. They'd place me in a nursing home before they'd invite me to live with them. And a nursing home, no matter how fine, is the last place I'd ever want to go."

Crystal sat up on the side of the lounge chair. "Oh, Etta, it won't come to that. Adam wouldn't allow such a thing."

"No," she said, then cut her eyes toward Crystal in a knowing way, "unless he marries a woman who doesn't want me around."

"But, Etta, isn't this your house? Your estate?"

"Legally, yes. But Adam controls it. It will be his someday. And it would be the simplest thing in the world to have me declared incompetent."

"Adam wouldn't do that to you," Crystal objected.

"He could be made to think it was best for me. And I just couldn't cope with *her*."

"Her?"

Etta nodded. "Elise. He's never loved anyone else. Now she's back. And she's going to be divorced. You heard her," she said, looking over at Crystal again. "There's only one reason she would come here, after eight years. And that reason is Adam."

Crystal stared at the ground in front of her.

"You wouldn't stay if Adam married Elise, would you?"

Crystal didn't know how to answer her. "That's not a consideration. I'm here for *you*. For you only. I've told you over and over."

"I know what you've told me. And what you tell yourself. But I also know what I see in your eyes, child. You're quite transparent. And Adam doesn't know what to do with you, for you are so moralistic and claim to be in love with that young man of yours."

Crystal was shaking her head. "You're making those insinuations again. The kind . . . I won't tolerate."

"If they were so ridiculous, you'd pass them off like you do other things I say. I could see it that very first night. And I knew Adam saw something different in you, too. I thought maybe—"

Unable to sit still any longer, Crystal sprang to her feet. "Maybe it's because I reminded him of Elise. And I'm not immune to the fact that Adam is a very attractive man. But I could never seriously consider a man who's not a Christian. It would be too . . . heartbreaking."

"Then you would stay, even if he married Elise?"

"I ... don't know, Etta. It depends on many things, one of them being whether or not she'd want me here."

"See?" Etta said accusingly. "It's not your decision. Nor mine. Nor Adam's. The decision is *hers*. And I know she hates Africa. She's afraid of it. She'll have Adam packed up and moved to London before you know it."

Crystal could see the possibilities. "But, couldn't you stay here at Shelomoh? You could hire people to take care of you."

"Oh, no," she said. "They'd never let me stay. Africa is too far from London, they'd say. No, for eight years, someone else has made all my decisions for me, and these past few weeks can't undo all that. That suicide attempt will always be held against me. I don't have the strength to assert myself ... not if *you* leave."

Crystal could not bear the look of vulnerability in Etta's demeanor as she sat slumped in her chair. But she lifted her head at last. "You've planted a seed of hope in me, child. But all seeds do not grow into tall plants. Doesn't your Bible say that some take root for a short while, then wither and die?"

Crystal knelt beside her and took her hand. "That doesn't have to happen to you."

"Doesn't it?" Etta asked, then suggested, "Perhaps we can talk further. Will you have dinner with us tonight?"

"Not tonight," Crystal murmured, and Etta didn't press.

"You look lovely, Etta," Crystal said as she helped the woman get ready for dinner. "And there's no reason why you can't stand up for yourself. This estate is yours. You have all the rights, sitting in that wheelchair, that you do standing on your own two feet. Now don't forget that."

"These three weeks with you have done me a world of good," Etta said distantly. "But they can't erase eight years of negative thinking."

"Then we'll keep trying," Crystal said. "I'll go down with you, if you like."

"No, thank you, dear. I have to start proving I can—" Etta paused, glancing up at her—"stand on my own two feet?"

Tears of emotion sprang to Crystal's eyes. "Ask God for strength. He'll give it to you."

Etta looked skeptical, but didn't respond. "Let's skip our reading for tonight. Neither of us will be in the mood."

Crystal's dinner was sent up on a tray, and there was nothing at all to indicate that Adam insisted she join them. Everything was different now. The "lovely little little dimpled blond" had no place at Adam's dinner table now that the great love of his life was back.

Crystal picked at her food and turned the television on to distract herself from her thoughts. Then she turned the lights out early and lay in bed, wondering how she could expect to be of help to Etta Sutherland when her own problems were growing out of all proportion.

For a long time she listened to the drums and, for the first time, found them disturbing rather than exciting. *She's back, she's back, she's back,* they throbbed. *Adam will not have to search for her in every blond he sees anymore.*

Crystal's pillow was wet. A nagging headache had returned, and she got up to take some medication, then returned to bed, and soon fell into a deep sleep, plagued by frightening dreams.

Opening her eyes and stretching luxuriously, Crystal turned her head toward the window . For one horrified moment, she thought she must still be dreaming. The instant she realized she was not, she sat bolt upright in bed.

She didn't know she'd screamed loudly enough for anyone else to hear, but apparently she had, for Bari appeared at her doorway immediately. "What wrong?" she asked. Then she gasped, seeing it, too, and placed her hand over her mouth.

On the other pillow beside Crystal lay a voodoo doll, its long hair streaming wildly about its face!

"Don't touch!" Bari exclaimed. "Stay there. I be back."

In a moment Etta wheeled herself to the doorway. A penetrating alarm was going off throughout the house.

"Somebody's just playing a little joke," Crystal said. "I'm not afraid of it. See?" She picked up the doll.

"Hmph! Around here it's no joke. Turn that thing off," Etta ordered Bari. "I'm sure it's been heard all the way to Umtali by now."

Bari hurried to obey.

"It's nothing," Crystal objected, pulling on a robe. "Let's don't make a fuss about it."

By that time, however, the other women were coming from their room. When they appeared at the doorway, Elise let out a bone-chilling shriek when she saw the doll. Adam got off the elevator and joined them, all crowding into the bedroom.

"Really," Crystal pleaded, "this is just a harmless doll. I can take a joke. I'm not at all frightened of a silly thing like this."

"Those things are serious," Elise said shakily, standing behind Gwen. She clutched her robe close to her throat.

"Somebody around here is practicing voodoo, and that's no joke."

"Oh," Etta waved her hand airily, "nobody in *this* house, I daresay." She peered into the faces of her staff. "Do you?"

Lalani and Bari nervously denied it. But Kudsai was nowhere to be seen. Crystal felt a shiver go down her spine to think that *someone*, maybe Kudsai, had crept upstairs in the dark of the night, head held high, big black eyes smoldering, and laid the doll on her pillow while she slept.

"We cannot treat this lightly," Adam said finally. "At the very least, it represents an invasion of privacy. We must regard it as a threat. And I intend to get to the bottom of it."

thirteen

When the others left the room, Adam stayed behind. He walked over to the bed, picked up the doll, and stared at it for a long moment.

"Adam," Crystal began slowly, seeing the dark look on his face, "surely you don't believe all this nonsense about . . . a cloth doll?"

"Not this *thing*, no," he replied. "But what is in the mind of the person who did it is quite a serious matter. You must understand the implication, and even the power behind something like this."

Yes, she could understand that. If someone called upon the powers of evil, they would be available. The doll symbolized that evil.

"But it's not wearing any of my belongings," she protested. "Surely nobody meant any harm." She looked helplessly at Adam. Could someone dislike her so much?

"We can't take a chance. I'll return you to the mission station as soon after breakfast as you can be ready."

Her mouth dropped open. "But what about my job? My responsibility to your mother? What about her?"

"Right now, I'm thinking of *you*," he said blandly. "Let me know when you're ready."

"But I can't leave her. She needs me. Now, more than ever," Crystal pleaded. "What happened to letting your mother make the decisions, Adam?"

He shook his head. "We all know that's not really the

143

way things are."

"Yes, we know, don't we?" came a harsh voice from the doorway. It was Etta. She turned abruptly and wheeled herself back into her own bedroom. Adam, holding the doll, strode after her.

"Two minutes, Mr. Sutherland!" Crystal called.

In the doorway, he stopped and turned around. "Eat your breakfast first."

"It might be poisoned!" she retorted. "And if you're not ready to take me back in two minutes, I'll walk. No, I won't," she retracted immediately. "I'll take the Bentley. I still have the keys, you know."

Without another word, Adam went into his mother's bedroom. Shortly Crystal could hear their voices raised in anger while she put on the ugliest thing she had—the green safari suit—brushed her hair straight back, and twisted it into a knot. She quickly brushed her teeth and splashed water on her face and dried it.

After grabbing her canvas bag, Crystal went to Etta's room. Adam was still there.

Ignoring him, Crystal knelt and took Etta's hands. "I love you," she said tearfully. "I want to stay here with you. But you can find the strength and the will for what we've planned. And remember, even if you never walk, I love you anyway. Here."

She handed Etta the key to the medicine cabinet. There were a dozen ways Etta could manage it, if she really wanted to commit suicide. "Give it to Bari, or do whatever you want with it."

"You'll be back," Etta said desperately.

"You know I can't if I'm not wanted here. But I'll find a way to keep in touch."

"This should not have happened," Etta groaned. "No matter how things look, please believe that I love you, too, child." A wrenching sob shook her body, and Crystal hurried from the room.

Adam rode down the elevator with her, but she kept her face turned toward the wall. "I'll be just a minute," he said, when the door opened at the first floor.

Crystal thought of going to the kitchen and accusing Kudsai of trying to frighten her. But that would be pointless. The dark-skinned woman would only deny it. She turned down the hallway and went out to the carport, got into the passenger seat of the Bentley, then leaned over to put the keys in the ignition.

Taking a deep breath, she warned herself to resist giving in to her swirling emotions. There would be time for that when she got to the mission station.

Presently, Adam rushed onto the carport, looked about frantically, then noticed her sitting in the car. When he got in, shirttail hanging out and ankles bare above his Nikes, he placed a check in her hand, then started the engine.

Crystal glanced at the huge sum, then tore the check into small pieces and let them filter to the floorboard.

Neither spoke until they were high in the air.

"Aren't you afraid the evil spirits are with us?" Crystal broke the long silence.

He looked over at her. "It's the *human* spirit that bothers me. When you don't know your enemy, you're a prime target."

"I've never had an enemy in my life," she muttered.

"Apparently you do now."

"Like I said, it's probably a joke. Maybe . . . maybe it

was Lalani, getting even for my spying on her in the trees. Young people often act without thinking of the consequences."

"It isn't likely that anybody, except you, believes we were out there spying on Lalani."

She looked out at the mounds of fluffy white clouds, like meringue on a pie. The sun was shining so innocently on the valleys below. How could everything be so beautiful outside, and so turbulent inside the plane?

"We saw her with her young man anyway," Crystal said finally. "That could be reason enough."

"Possibly," he said. "Who else?"

She stared at him, wondering if he were really serious. She might as well play his game. "George," she said. "He was embarrassed because he came out in his pajamas, holding a gun."

Adam didn't laugh, but issued her a warning glance.

"Well then, it has to be Kudsai. I don't know the reason, but you do. Surely you haven't forgotten the night the lights went out."

He nodded, but did not elaborate. "What about Bari?"

She had to think a little while on that one. "OK. Maybe she's afraid her daughter will get in trouble because of her tryst in the jungle, so she's getting even. Or that Etta will come to depend on me instead of her."

"Mmmm. And Gwen?"

"Gwen," she repeated, with sudden seriousness. "Your mother told her that *I* treat her like a daughter, implying that Gwen does not. I know that remark really hurt your sister."

A long moment passed, then he asked, "Elise?"

Crystal didn't want to play the game anymore. But she

couldn't very well refuse. "Easy. She heard you say you wanted me to stay . . . permanently, and in her frustration over losing her husband and finding you again, she was . . . jealous."

At least, he didn't laugh.

"That leaves Mother," he said.

Crystal wanted to get it over with, then she hoped they could change the subject. "There could be only one reason. Etta would want to scare me away, because . . . because she doesn't want to try anymore."

"That's the closest you've come to the truth," he said.

"On the other hand, she knows I wouldn't be frightened by a doll."

"But she knows *I* would whisk you away from there," Adam countered, "if I thought someone was threatening you."

Crystal wished the scenario did not sound so plausible. "This is all ridiculous," she said. "You couldn't possibly believe my life is in danger. Maybe someone dislikes me. Maybe they wanted to frighten me. But . . . *kill* me?" She gave a short, harsh laugh. "No, Adam. Maybe *you* wanted me away from the house for some reason. That's it!" she said with sudden inspiration. "*You* put that doll on my pillow!"

"Why would I do such a thing?"

Out of desperation, she stated Etta's worst fears. "You wanted me out of the way so you and Elise could put your mother in a home, and take control of her possessions."

"I could have done that eight years ago. Or even *two* years ago, after she tried to commit suicide," he replied. "And I could do it now, whether or not you were at the house."

"Yes, but with two blonds underfoot, your integrity might be in question."

"Ah," he said, again glancing at her with a devious gleam in his eye. "That remark has the ring of jealousy about it."

"Are you implying I'm jealous of Elise?"

"No," he said, "*you* did."

Her first impulse was to deny it. But after a slight hesitation, she admitted, "Maybe I was. I enjoyed being the center of attention." Suddenly she felt a sense of embarrassment, then outrage that she had permitted herself to be drawn into his little game. "This is ridiculous! You've put these hypothetical questions to me, and I've answered them as if they were reality. I'm not jealous!"

"It's all right. I understand," Adam said quietly. "It's a bit like I feel about David Hamilton. You see, I haven't exactly been without my admirers. Yet you've talked about David constantly. I've found myself asking what this man has that is so appealing."

"It certainly isn't his possessions," she suggested with mock helpfulness. "And I'm sure your many admirers have given you a clue as to your physical charm—" She paused. "I think you know David's most appealing quality, as far as I'm concerned. And Adam," she added gently, "it's available to anyone, and it's free. Surrendering to Jesus Christ will be the best investment you'll ever make."

"Crystal," he replied doggedly, "there is one thing I would never do. And that is to pretend a religious faith in order to please a woman. I wouldn't go that far. In spite of your friend Jess saying that men would do almost anything for you."

Jess again! What in the world was that girl trying to do? "We've gotten off the subject," she said. "What about the doll?"

"Let's see," he mused. "Oh, yes. *You* did it, because you were jealous and wanted attention drawn to yourself."

She knew by the bantering tone of his voice that he wasn't serious. But his next question *was*. "Why didn't you join us for dinner last night?"

"I—I had a headache," she said. "Besides, I didn't want to intrude on a family gathering."

"Elise isn't family," he returned.

But she will be, Crystal was thinking as the plane touched down on the landing strip at Sanyati. *Elise is at Shelomoh and I'm going back to the mission station.*

After the plane taxied to a stop, Adam turned to face her. "I know who did it."

She stared at him. She might never see him again. There were so many things she longed to say at this moment, but it was too late. "Who?"

A painful expression clouded his eyes and he looked out at the familiar landscape. "Once, when Dr. Kent came to the house years ago, he brought a Bible and a voodoo doll. He used those two items to illustrate the choices we could make in life. Symbols of good and evil, life and death."

He paused, and his dark eyes locked with Crystal's. "Mother wanted nothing to do with them, so I told her they would be in the bottom drawer of my desk, in case she ever wanted them."

Crystal closed her eyes against his intense gaze. The picture of Etta sitting in Adam's study that morning flashed through her mind. She opened her eyes and stared at her hands while he added, "She and I are the only ones with a key to the desk."

Her eyes slowly sought his, hoping for any slight chance that he was wrong. "Perhaps someone broke in."

"I checked before I left the house."

She moistened her lips. "Somebody could have stolen her key. Or had a duplicate made."

"That's true," Adam agreed. "But highly unlikely."

"Then maybe . . . she *did* do it," Crystal acknowledged with great sadness, remembering Etta's last words to her. "She could have had Bari slip in and put it on my pillow. But you know what this means, Adam," she continued with a growing sense of desperation. "Her action wasn't against *me*, it was against *herself!* She's planning to do something terrible!"

He nodded in agreement. "I know. And it's time we handled this matter together, as a family. With Gwen here, perhaps we can do that."

She reached over and grasped his arm. "Oh, Adam," she said fearfully, "please don't put Etta in a home. That would be the end for her. If it comes to that, let me stay with her. I'll take care of her."

Her trapped her small hand beneath his large one. "I'm her son, Crystal. I love my mother, and I'll do what I think is best for her."

"But we don't always know what's best. I'm more objective."

"Are you?" he asked. "You've become part of us, Crystal. Like I said to Gwen, I'd like for you to stay forever. But that's part of the reason why you should *leave*."

She knew she'd been wrong to allow her emotions to overrule her professionalism. "You don't want me to go back?" she asked in a whisper.

"I don't know," he replied. "First, I have to try and discover why Mother did this thing. You've completely lost your objectivity if you think this is normal behavior."

"Normal," she repeated scornfully. "Oh, Adam. Don't try to make her prove she's normal. Who can do that?" She wriggled her hand free. "It was a foolish mistake. Everybody makes them."

A Land Rover appeared. Adam opened the door, got out, and held out his hand to assist her. "I'll be in touch as soon as I learn what's going on." He looked toward the vehicle where Jess sat waiting. "Tell your friend she was right about you."

Before Crystal could pursue the matter, he turned abruptly, climbed back into the cockpit, and slammed the door shut. When the engine caught, she stepped away and hurried to the Land Rover.

"Are you all right, Crys?" Jess asked anxiously.

"All right?" Crystal replied. "I doubt that I'll ever be all right again."

"I couldn't imagine what had happened when Gwen called and said someone should meet you at the landing strip. But you look OK. Where are your things?"

"I left in too big a hurry to get them. Perhaps someone will drop them off." She looked up toward the sky, as if halfway expecting them to be dropped from a plane.

"Tell me all about it," Jess urged, "and don't leave out a thing."

"Oh, Jess. It wouldn't surprise me to discover you flew to the estate, sneaked in, and put that voodoo doll on my pillow yourself, just to stir up some excitement."

"A voodoo doll . . . on your pillow? Oh, Crys, how

thrilling!" Jess could hardly keep the Land Rover on the narrow dirt road. Her eyes danced with delight. "I told Adam that wherever you are, the intrigue is unbelievable, and you've proven me right again!"

When Crystal didn't respond, Jessica rattled on. "Someday you can tell your children all about the estate in the Umtali Mountains, where this rich and handsome man swept you away into the jungle late at night, and the narrow escape you had!" She looked over at her friend, only to find a trail of tears staining her cheeks. "Crys, Crys, honey, what's the matter?"

"I failed, Jess! I should be there, and I'm here. Etta needs me, but planned to get rid of me. Adam wants me to stay forever, and kicks me out. Oh, Jess, I'm so confused!"

"Go on, honey, have a good cry," she said, bringing the Land Rover to a stop under the carport. "I'll get ready for work, and then we can talk."

fourteen

"*Kwashiorkor!*"

Crystal stirred from the couch in Jess's apartment where she had been crying and dabbed at her eyes. "What did you say?"

"Measles," Jess translated. "Dr. Kent just called and said a child was brought in last night from a tribe outside Mujiba. She's dead, Crystal. And many others are sick. We're spreading the word that we'll be giving free shots at the clinic."

"Can I help?" Crystal asked, her own problems temporarily forgotten.

"We'll need all the help we can get. I'll go on to the clinic and have someone bring you a uniform. Come as soon as you're ready."

As quickly as possible, Crystal showered and changed, slipping into the pink uniform brought by a school girl.

On her way to the clinic, she saw some African women filing in from all directions, balancing bundles, covered by bright-colored scarves on their heads. Babies were attached securely to their mothers' backs, while small children skipped along beside them, followed by a gaggle of goats and dogs.

They'd come prepared to spend the day in line, if necessary. And from the looks of the crowd, it would be a very *long* day. The people were divided into three lines, with Jess, her assistant, and Crystal administering the immunizations. Older students from the school assisted with supplies and office needs, and held the children's hands while they had their shots. Others organized games outside for those who were waiting.

By nightfall, they were ready for a break. With Jess's Land Rover now being used to transport doctors and nurses out into the outlying villages, Crystal and Jessica walked the few blocks to her apartment.

"We can't force them to get their shots," Jess said with concern, "but many just won't come to us until an emergency drives them out of the bush."

At the apartment, Jess made coffee while Crystal dished up the food sent by the cafeteria staff.

"It's frightening," Jess went on. "The people who live away from the cities are so protein-deficient that the children have almost no resistance. Measles, or any other disease, can spread quickly and wipe out an entire area."

"That's why your mother's work is so important," Crystal said, thinking of Clara's experiments in nutrition.

Jess sat down at the table, across from Crystal. "A lot of progress has been made," she admitted, "but education of the bush people is a near impossibility. You've seen some of the roads, if you can call them that. Too often, the diseases get to the people before *we* do."

Jess studied the table, laden with food. "Do you know what some of the nearby villagers eat for protein?" she asked, just as Crystal lifted a forkful of stewed chicken to her mouth.

Crystal shook her head.

"Termites!" Jess explained.

Crystal glanced at her bite of chicken and choked. "You don't want me to enjoy my supper, do you?"

Jess laughed. "You'd better eat hearty. You'll need

your strength. We'll be giving shots all day tomorrow, too."

"At least I'm where I can be useful," Crystal said wistfully, blinking back the the hot moisture starting in her eyes.

A knock sounded on the door. "Come in," Jess invited, too tired to move.

"David!" they said in unison as the tall sandy-haired man stepped into the kitchen.

"So you recognized me underneath all this road dirt?" His face, arms, and clothes were streaked with it.

"Where have you been?" Crystal wanted to know.

"In the bush. Missionaries have to be versatile here, you know."

"So do your students, apparently," Crystal replied. "They were lifesavers today, David."

"When something like this happens, fortunately not too often, we cancel the higher classes and put the students to work. Several went into the bush with us. They're invaluable interpreters. Oh . . . here."

David took a folded envelope from his back pocket and handed it to Crystal. "Sorry about the fingerprints," he apologized.

Crystal took it, staring at the familiar crest. "Where'd you get this?"

"Adam asked me to give it to you. Said it was your salary."

She laid it on the corner of the table, then turned her head away so David wouldn't see the quick tears welling up again.

Jess glanced at her, then at David. "Where did you run into him?"

"The estate," David explained. "He and Dr. Kent had a telephone conversation before noon, and when Dr. Kent told him about the epidemic, Adam offered us the use of his plane. There aren't too many places to land out in the bush, of course, so a plane is a real novelty. The folks know when our small planes land that we have something good for them—medicine, food during a dry spell, or a treat for the children before we present the Gospel. The same with Adam. They know which government officials are for or against them. Adam's irrigation project and his land-rights bill make him relatively safe and respected."

"Then you reached most of the people today?" Jess asked.

David nodded. "We were able to get into most of the remote areas, and had the plane back to Adam by this afternoon. This," he said, holding out his dirty shirt by the tail, "came afterwards, when we borrowed their Land Rover and went into the outskirts of Umtali." He sighed. "There's still some distrust of the mission, even outright hatred, among the people here."

"Isn't that terribly dangerous, David?" Crystal asked, then answered the question herself. "Of course it is. That's what missionary work is all about. Giving of yourself to others, regardless of the danger."

David shrugged. "Suppose I get cleaned up, then come back later, and we'll talk."

"We've both had a long day," Crystal said gently. "Maybe tomorrow."

"Sure." He frowned, puzzled. "Call me if you change your mind."

After David left, a full half-minute passed before Jess said, "One of us is going to read that letter to me."

"*You* read it," Crystal said, then slapped her hand over it as Jess reached. "Never mind, I'll do it." She opened the envelope. Inside was a check for the same amount as the one she'd torn up earlier. The few words scrawled on the notepaper read: "Crystal. I'll call this evening. Adam."

She handed it to Jess, who gave her a knowing look. "Did you read between the lines?"

"Oh, Jess. There is no between-the-lines."

"With a check like that?"

"It's a goodbye check," Crystal insisted. "Elise is there."

"Elise?" Jess questioned. "Adam's former fiancée?"

Crystal nodded.

"No wonder you're upset!" Jess exploded. "The woman tried to put a spell on you with that voodoo doll!"

Crystal rolled her eyes toward the ceiling. "Jess, I'm upset because Etta Sutherland has decided not to continue with our plans. She'll try to do something terrible to herself, but to prevent it, Adam and Gwen will put her in a sanatorium somewhere, which will destroy her as surely as if she had taken her own life." She spread her hands. "I'm helpless to do anything."

"Tell me about it," Jess said. "But let's go in the living room and get comfortable. I have the feeling it's going to be a long story."

It was after nine when the phone rang. Jess answered it. "Yes, Adam, she's here."

"You received my note?" he asked Crystal when Jess handed her the receiver and stepped into the kitchen to give them some privacy.

"Yes."

"Mother explained why she had Bari put that doll on your pillow." He paused. "She said she did it to frighten Elise. I'm afraid that doesn't make good sense."

"Oh, it makes *perfect* sense, Adam."

"You believe her?" he asked, incredulity in his voice.

"Of course. I should have known. That's why she had Bari sound the alarm—so everyone would know."

He exhaled audibly. "I thought perhaps those were the ramblings of a senile woman, and that I should try and placate her. Anyway," he continued, "it was apparent she did not want Elise there, so I sent her to Oleta's in Umtali."

"How wonderful! I—I mean, for your mother," Crystal quickly added, "since . . . that's what she wants."

"Now," he said, "about us. Gwen, Mother, and I are talking things out, some of which has waited eight years to be said. There's been a lot of suppressed heartache and misunderstanding in this family, and we're trying to deal with it, Crystal."

"So you don't know if or when you want me to return?"

"I know *if*—" his voice was warm and tender—"but not *when*. Maybe in a few days. I'll be in touch. Good night, Crystal."

"Good night, Adam."

"You're positively glowing, Crys," Jess said, coming into the room with a pot of coffee and two cups. "What happened?"

"Didn't you hear?" Crystal asked accusingly.

"Not *his* side of the conversation," Jess replied innocently.

"Oh, Jess, I should have known why Etta had Bari put that doll on my pillow. It would be too risky to go to the third floor and slip into Elise's room. My bedroom door stays ajar in case Etta calls me in the night. And she knew it wouldn't scare *me* away, but hoped it would scare *Elise* into leaving."

"Slow down," Jess said. "Now tell it all."

Crystal told her about Etta's fears of being put in a home, losing complete control of the estate, being moved to London.

"So now everything's working out just perfectly, isn't it, Crys?" Jess said brightly. "You'll go back and help Etta until she walks again. Adam will regain his lost love. You'll marry David and find your purpose at the clinic or in the bush. I'll marry Robert. He'll take that position in Salisbury, and we'll all live happily ever after. Right?"

Crystal looked at Jess over the rim of her coffee cup, then set it down. "Sure looks that way."

"Amazing how things turn out," Jess added.

"Yeah," Crystal said distantly.

fifteen

By Saturday, the crowds, coming for immunization, had dwindled. It was a particularly hot day, and when David suggested a swim, Crystal, Jess, and Robert eagerly agreed.

Crystal borrowed a swimsuit from a nurse who was about her size, and they soon reached the swimming hole, five miles from the mission station.

"This is the life," Crystal sighed, floating on her back in the cool water and gazing up at a cloudless sky.

"Yeah, I needed this," Jess agreed. "I was beginning to smell like a goat."

Crystal laughed and shot her a confirming glance. She'd been reluctant to mention that the hot morning, in combination with an assortment of persons who had slept all night with goats and dogs, had provided a new experience in aromas!

She draped a towel around her shoulders, climbed up on the rocks, and sat watching the others dive off them, plunging into the water below. Soon, David joined her, shaking the water like a boisterous pup, before he toweled himself dry and sat down.

Crystal smiled at him. This outing with friends, the cool water, the mid afternoon sun—all of it was beginning to work its magic, reducing the tension of the past two days.

"You made quite a hit with the hospital staff, Crystal," David complimented her. "You could have a job there if you wanted one. Also," he added, "if Robert takes the position in Salisbury, Jess will probably go with him, which would leave the assistant directorship open at the Well Baby Clinic."

Such a possibility was very real. "Then I could do what Jess has wanted all along, and stay in Africa—" Her voice trailed off. She had almost added, "forever." Instead, she pulled her knees up to her chest, hugged them, and looked at her wiggling toes.

The towel slipped from her shoulders. "I'll turn into a beet if I'm not careful," she said, reaching for it to pull it around her.

David reached at the same time and kept his arm around her even after her shoulders were safely covered. With the other hand, he guided her chin until she was facing him. His moist lips touched hers in the whisper of a kiss. But there was something about it that seemed to bother David. Backing away a little to look at her, he searched her eyes, then settled back again, still holding her lightly.

"Amazing, isn't it," he said, focusing on the figures in the water below, "that Robert, normally so staid and proper, even stuffy, could become that frolicking, playful guy down there? All because of Jess."

Crystal nodded and smiled, watching them. Kissing, while dog-paddling, couldn't be the easiest thing in the world.

"Why aren't we doing something like that?" David asked wistfully.

Her glance told her he was not being playful. His eyes held an unusual seriousness. "I'm sorry if I'm not very good company today, David. I've had a lot of things on my mind recently."

"You had a problem at the Sutherlands," he said, "but you can't tell me about it."

She almost agreed with him, but the thought flashed through her mind that she and David should share everything. "Of course I can. Etta put a voodoo doll on my pillow," she began, and quickly summarized the story.

David nodded when she had finished. "So you're returning to the estate?"

"Yes," Crystal said, explaining, "Etta needs me. Such wonderful things are beginning to happen with her."

David was quiet. Then he said a strange thing. "It's hard to imagine you and me, living in the States . . . you the wife of a pastor of a small church somewhere . . . a little girl and boy underfoot—"

"That sounds . . . wonderful."

"I know," he said. "There's only one thing missing. You're not in love with me. Now wait," he added quickly when she opened her mouth to protest, "that's not a condemnation. Just an observation."

"David," she replied honestly, "there's every reason to love you."

He nodded. "That's what everybody tells me. My greatest problem has been waiting for love to come my way. I try to push it, make it happen. I'm sorry," he said quickly. "It's just a mood. Let's swim."

David walked to the edge of the rocks, poised for a dive. Robert and Jess began to yell at him, gesticulating wildly. At first, Crystal thought they were playing, then recognized the fear in Jess's voice. David executed the dive, landing in the shallow water at the edge of the swimming hole. He lay there, face down, unmoving.

Quickly Jess and Robert swam over to David, while

Crystal clambered down the rocks as fast as she could, Robert instructing them on how to move David very carefully, only far enough to keep his face out of the water.

"There's no telephone between here and the mission station, Jess. You'll have to go for the ambulance," Robert said. "Crystal, find something to cover him."

The two women raced to the Land Rover. "He was on the wrong rock for diving!" Jess wailed. "How could he have made such a mistake? He's been here before."

It wasn't a question Crystal could answer. She grabbed their clothes and towels. Jess jumped under the steering wheel and sped away.

Crystal could see that Robert was sitting in the water, bracing David's body to prevent any movement. "The water will help support his weight," he said, when she ran up with the items. "Spread the towels over him to keep the sun off. We'll try to keep him as comfortable as possible."

Crystal stared at the strange angle of David's back and looked fearfully at Robert. "Don't speculate," he said. "Just pray." She spread the towels over his back and shoulders, feeling the air cooling as the sun sank lower. David's head, too, seemed oddly twisted, his face in the wet sand, with Robert's hand underneath his nose and mouth.

"Let me help," Crystal said, hoping to protect the surgeon's hands. He nodded, and she moved into place beside him, working quickly to slip her own hands into the proper position.

Fun-loving, happy, outgoing, wonderful David, she thought, scarcely able to believe what was happening. *How could he have done such a silly thing?* Why had he suddenly dived off that rock? Was it their conversation?

Was it her fault? She shook her head, her mind reeling. She mustn't think like that. At least he was breathing. She could feel the moist warmth of his breath on her hand.

The wail of a siren was followed at last by the flashing lights of the ambulance, coming to a halt right behind Jess's Land Rover.

Robert stood by to supervise David's move onto a stretcher. "We're not equipped to handle this kind of injury at the mission station," he told Jess, putting on his clothes over his wet bathing suit. "We'll have to take him to Salisbury. You'd better call ahead, then come whenever you can make arrangements to leave the mission." He told her what emergency treatment might be needed.

"I'll call Dad and let him know you're coming," Jessica promised, as he jumped into the ambulance behind David's stretcher. He closed the doors and the ambulance moved away.

Crystal and Jessica followed in the Land Rover, Jess at the wheel, slowing for the deep ruts. "There's nothing we can do right now except pray, Crys," Jessica said, seeing Crystal's stricken face. "We're going to have to think rationally, not emotionally."

"I know." At the moment, however, Crystal was drained of all emotion. She could only watch the red taillights of the ambulance preceding them down the narrow road, praying that David would live, until the vehicle turned off onto the road to Salisbury.

When the two women reached the mission station, there were a million details to attend to. While Jessica called her father to alert him to the tragedy, Crystal discussed the incident with Dr. Kent.

"He'll have the best of care at the hospital in Salisbury," the doctor spoke reassuringly. "Let's just take it one step at a time. The first thing is to get hold of yourself," he told Crystal, observing her anxious face. "We need you calm and collected for . . . whatever is ahead."

When Jess hung up, she and Dr. Kent mapped out a list of priorities. The duties seemed endless—Robert's rounds, visitors coming to the clinic on Sunday, the measles inoculations. And David's students and the other teachers must to be told of his accident, not to mention the mission board . . . and his parents. Rumors would already be flying. Not only that, but prayer meetings should be set up for David.

With Robert away, and one of the planes and crew still out in the bush, they were already seriously understaffed. Jess took a deep breath, then exhaled slowly. "I had planned to go with you to Salisbury," she told Crystal, "but there's just no way I can leave right now. You understand—"

"From what I hear—" there was a twinkle in Dr. Kent's eye—"*you're* not the one David will be wanting to see when he comes around. It's Crystal here. But with his injury, I suspect it will be at least tomorrow before *anyone* can see him." He turned to regard Crystal over his spectacles. "Perhaps by then, someone will be free to drive you down—"

"I'll take care of that." It was Adam! Who had called him, Crystal wondered, flustered, but relieved to see him.

There was a hurried conference with Dr. Kent, and before she knew it, the decision had been made for Crystal to return with Adam to Shelomoh, where they'd await word from Dr. Cliburn when visitors would be allowed.

She was so numb by that time that she was barely aware of stopping by Jess's apartment for a quick shower and change of clothes before their short flight.

In the air on the way to Shelomoh, Crystal finally remembered her manners. "It's good of you to do this. Help out the way you have. Loaning your plane to the mission. Offering your services. You're a good man, Adam."

"It's the least I can do, Crystal. We have our different ways of showing it, but I care about Africa and its people as much as Dr. Kent and the others at the mission. And *you*—" he turned to look at her—"what *you* have brought into all our lives can't be measured."

"Oh, Adam, when I found out that Etta had had Bari put that doll on my pillow, I thought I'd failed completely."

"No," he said emphatically. "The failure is not yours. But Crystal," he added, "Mother *is* responding. I know it's too soon to be overly optimistic, but we've talked as we haven't in over eight years."

As he told her about Etta's progress, Adam's excitement mounted. "Mother is asserting herself. It's painful, for all of us, but wonderful to see. It's the sort of thing the psychiatrists had hoped for years ago. We're finally being honest with each other."

At the house, Gwen met them at the door with a message from Dr. Cliburn. "You're to call as soon as possible," she told Adam.

While Adam placed the call in the study, Gwen led Crystal into the drawing room. "Mother will be down in a minute," she said, glancing toward the doorway. "So let me take this opportunity to thank you. I feel I'm getting my mother back—" She broke off when Etta wheeled into the room.

"Oh, child, I'm so sorry about your David," she said after Crystal had given her a quick hug. "How is he?"

"We don't know yet," she said with a little catch in her voice. "Adam's talking with Dr. Cliburn now."

When Adam joined them, his face was pale, his eyes dark with concern. "David has two fractured vertebrae and a dislocated spinal column," he said, coming to the point quickly. "But Robert is with him, and everything possible is being done for him."

"His neck—" Crystal began, remembering the distorted twist of his head as he lay in the water.

"His neck is not broken, but there is swelling, and he's having some respiratory distress. He—he's still unconscious. They'll know more when he comes to."

"If there's anything we can do—" Gwen took Crystal's hand.

"Yes, child, it's our turn to help," Etta spoke up. "You've become one of us, almost like family. If you want to talk, or cry, or be alone—"

"And we expect you to rely on that faith you've preached to us," Adam said, not unkindly, with a smile of encouragement.

Crystal looked into their compassionate faces. How could she tell them the truth about David? She drew a deep breath. "I don't want to mislead you," she began, and glanced from one to the other. "I am greatly concerned about David, but his life is out of my hands. It's too big for me, and I know that. No," she affirmed adamantly, "my faith in God has not wavered. It's—" she paused before reluctantly admitting—"it's my own guilt that's bothering me."

"Guilt?" Etta asked. "Whyever would you feel guilty, child?"

"David and I had a misunderstanding right before the accident. So I feel that . . . it may have been my fault."

They waited patiently, not asking the obvious questions that begged an answer, while Crystal regained her composure.

"You see, David could have been upset over our conversation and misjudged the diving spot. The rock he dived from was only about ten feet high, and he dived too close to the edge of the swimming hole into about two feet of water—"

Adam was incredulous. "You mean, you think he risked his life . . . on purpose? Jessica was right. You *do* have a devastating effect on men."

She looked at him fearfully, hearing the condemnation in his tone and shook her head in desperation. "I should never have come to Africa! I've made such a mess of things!"

"Now, now," Etta soothed, "everything will look better when you've had a chance to rest. We'll talk more after supper."

The first thing Etta did over supper in her sitting room was to apologize to Crystal for causing the problem with the voodoo doll. "You understand why I did it?"

Crystal, feeling somewhat calmer, was able to think more clearly. "You were exerting yourself, as I suggested, though it wasn't exactly what I had in mind."

"Well, it worked, didn't it?" Etta retorted, and Crystal could not resist a wry smile that dimpled her cheeks.

After supper, the conversation grew more intense. "You

must rid yourself of guilt, Crystal, not hold it inside," Etta advised. "Look what it's done to me."

A steely determination crept into Etta's voice. "I'm going to admit something I've never told anyone. The night Reggie died . . . the night of the accident . . . *I* was driving." A sense of relief seemed to sweep over her as the painful story unfolded. "I didn't realize that I've been punishing myself all these years because I'm alive . . . and Reggie isn't. You see, I didn't think I *deserved* to walk." She laid her hand on Crystal's arm. "You only hurt yourself—" she paused a moment, considering—"no, you also hurt those around you when you harbor such grief and remorse and guilt."

Crystal did not reply that her sense of guilt was no more than a mild regret that she and David had an unresolved situation between them. Etta was reaching out in a way she hadn't done in eight years—thinking, not of herself, but of someone else.   Crystal could say honestly, "Etta, I can't thank you enough. Your talking with me like this makes all the difference in the world."

Etta smiled. "Now, come with me."

Crystal followed her into the bedroom.

Etta wheeled herself over to the bed, reached over and put her weight on the bars of a walker, pulled herself from the chair, pushed the walker a couple of feet, then sat back on the bed with a broad smile.

"You should try such a thing!" Etta scolded mockingly, while Crystal stood with the tears running down her face.

"Oh, Etta," Crystal whispered and came over to sit on the floor at her feet.

"Now, I've fulfilled my part of the bargain," Etta said staunchly. "It's *your* turn."

Crystal looked up at her. "Bargain?"

Etta nodded. "You said if I would walk, you would stay. You just saw me take a couple of steps. Now, don't look so stricken. I know you have to go to David. He needs you now more than any of us. But you must promise that you'll be back."

Etta was right. David's needs took precedence over everything else at the moment. They would all have to do whatever was necessary for him. It might even mean her taking a job at the Salisbury hospital for a while.

What the future held, she couldn't know. But the thoughts of leaving the Sutherland estate behind cut deeply into her heart. She could not just walk away . . . as if a case were closed . . . as if a patient was on the way to a complete healing. As Etta had said, she had become a part of their family.

"Yes," Crystal admitted slowly. "I'll be back. I'll have to know—"

Etta nodded in understanding. "Now, would you have Bari come in. You must try to rest . . . and so must I."

Crystal went to her bedroom and stood for a moment at the window. Then her eye caught a movement beyond the pool. Adam and Gwen. After a moment, she turned and readied herself for bed. She probably wouldn't sleep, but Etta was right, she should try.

Far into the night she thought about her purpose in Africa. Perhaps it had been, as David said, for Etta Sutherland. Etta had taken her first steps. She'd continue to get well now that she'd found a way out of her emotional prison. The woman Adam had loved eight years ago was now in Umtali. He could resume that relationship if he wished.

As for me, Crystal thought, *it's time to go. I'm not needed here . . . permanently.*

sixteen

Crystal's immediate inclination upon awakening in her room at Shelomoh was to languish beneath the luxurious covers, breathe in the fragrant morning air, and touch the rays of sunshine streaking through the windows, making golden patterns on her bed.

The impulse vanished with her first coherent thought. *David*! She sat up in bed. "Has there been any word?" she asked Lalani, who brought coffee on a tray.

The girl shook her head. "Mr. Adam say he tell you when Dr. Cliburn call." She paused, then asked uncertainly, "You like breakfast?"

Crystal started to decline, saying that she didn't feel like eating. But there was something in Lalani's eyes that reminded her of herself, the many times she had wanted to do something to help, but had been unable to. "Yes," she replied, "I'd like that, thank you."

As soon as Lalani left the room, Crystal said a prayer for David, then threw back the covers and sipped her coffee while staring out the windows at the cloud-covered mountain peaks in the distance. She must keep busy, she reminded herself, not just sit here waiting for the telephone to ring.

By midmorning, dressed in a conservative beige sleeveless dress, Crystal walked out into the courtyard, wandering near the jacaranda tree, where the chameleon had played hide and seek a few mornings ago. It seemed like years.

"Crystal."

Her hair swung around her shoulders as she turned to acknowledge Adam's greeting, eager yet apprehensive.

"Let's go into my study," he invited.

Her heels clicked against the concrete as she hurried inside, dreading what he would tell her. She didn't take a seat, but walked to a window, moved the drape aside, and looked out. There were still parts of the estate she had not explored. Even parts of the house. Perhaps depths of her own heart. Now, there would not be a chance. Her thoughts must be only of David.

"William Cliburn called," Adam said needlessly. He breathed deeply, then continued, "Arrangements are underway to move David to the States."

"Why? What's happened?" Crystal asked, whirling to face him, not sure she wanted to hear the answer. "Can't they treat him at the Salisbury hospital?"

"His injuries, yes," Adam replied quietly. "But they do not have the advanced technology needed for his recovery."

She stared at him and he looked down at his fingers, moving absently in a pattern along the edge of the desk. "What's the diagnosis?" she dared to ask at last.

"David is . . . paralyzed."

She closed her eyes as if to shut out the grim words that would seal her fate.

"There's every reason to be optimistic, Crystal," Adam said reassuringly. "William said temporary paralysis was to be expected. David's young, in excellent physical condition. He may yet pull out of it."

Crystal understood the vague expressions all too well.

That's what doctors said when they really didn't *know* what to expect. "Is he still in a coma?"

"Yes," Adam admitted reluctantly. "The move was requested by David's family, as soon as it can be done safely. And William feels it's better for David to be moved now, rather than wait—"

"As soon as he regains consciousness, of course," Crystal amended.

"William expects that to be any time now." He gave her a long, steady look. "David has come out of the coma long enough to call your name."

"When does he leave?"

"We're working on that now," Adam said, running his fingers through his hair. "Mission Hospital, in the States, says they can be ready for David as soon as we can get him there. I'll try to pull a few strings, charter a jet—"

"Did William say that I could see David?"

Adam regarded her for another long moment before a shadow crossed his eyes. "Better than that. William said you may go with him."

"To the States?"

Adam nodded soberly "Robert will go along. He'll need an anesthetist and a nurse. We all thought that, under the circumstances, you'd want to be with him."

David had asked for her. She owed him that much. After all, she'd seen much of Africa. Had felt its heartbeat. And her purpose here had been fulfilled. David needed her now.

"I have to go," she said.

"Yes, of course, you do," Adam replied. He turned from her and placed his hand on the telephone. "I need to make some phone calls. We'll leave as soon as possible."

Adam made his phone calls, while she, Lalani, and Bari packed her belongings. Crystal put on a jacket that matched her dress, fastened the thin brown belt, and slipped in some gold earrings. Then came the moment she had dreaded. While the two African women dabbed at teary eyes, Adam put her luggage on the elevator. "I've talked with Dr. Kent," he said, as the door closed behind them. "It was decided that Jessica will go into Salisbury with us."

Crystal nodded. "We've barely had a chance to say hello," she said. "Now it's goodbye."

"That's why it's imperative that Jessica go. She wants to see you off, as well as say goodbye to Robert and David."

The door opened at the first floor. Adam began to remove the bags. Crystal went into the kitchen where Kudsai uttered a stiff farewell, looking as if she wanted to say more.

When they emerged from the house, Gwen and Etta were sitting at a shaded table in the courtyard, pouring over magazines and talking about renovations for the estate.

"You promised," Etta reminded Crystal when they hugged.

Crystal didn't trust herself to speak. "We'll keep in touch," she said emotionally.

Gwen drove them to the landing strip. "I'll be staying with Mother for a while," she said. "The family will probably come soon. It's wonderful, Crystal, being able to communicate with her again. I couldn't bear to see her so withdrawn, while we were helpless to do anything."

They arrived at the landing strip and Adam put her bags in the plane, then stood at the bottom of the steps while she and Gwen embraced. "We'd all like for you to return, Crystal," Gwen said sincerely. "I hope you know that."

Crystal could scarcely keep the tears back. "Thank you, Gwen. But David has to come first right now."

After the plane soared into the sky, Crystal looked back at the estate, nestled in the mountainous jungle, then along the Umtali Valley, until it faded from sight. "I'm going to miss it," she murmured.

"Incredible," Adam said, "how a lovely little dimpled blond could come on the scene, change everyone's lives so quickly, then poof! she's gone." He glanced at her. "All of us will miss you."

"Not *all* of you," she amended. "Kudsai doesn't like me."

"It's not that she doesn't like you. She just doesn't trust you."

"Why on earth not?" Crystal asked incredulously.

"She's rather like a member of the family," Adam explained patiently. "Her mother and father used to work for my parents, so she toddled around the house with me years ago. She warned me about you that very first night, while you were upstairs with Mother."

"She did?"

"Like everyone else," he went on, "Kudsai believes that Elise broke my heart. I don't know where she got her information, but she's convinced that American blonds are more fickle than English, and if I pursued you, my heart would be broken again."

"Well," Crystal said quickly, "she needn't have worried. I'm leaving. There's only one blond in your life now."

"You're right," he admitted. "There's only one."

"Is Elise still in Umtali?"

"Yes. She's waiting for that talk we've never gotten around to having," Adam said. "There hasn't been time—" He looked over at Crystal, then peered down at the ground far below. "There isn't time for us, either. We'll be landing soon."

Crystal felt a moment of panic. There was still so much she wanted to say to him. But what, and how?

"I'm going to admit something to you, Crystal," Adam was saying. "Mother is not the only one who experienced a crisis eight years ago. My life changed drastically, too. I lost my father. My mother became an invalid. My close relationship with a woman ended. And I stepped in to take my father's place in the home, business, community, and government."

Crystal listened carefully while Adam confessed his fears and insecurities during those days, when so many people were leaning on him, expecting him to be strong. "It hasn't been easy for me. But I've learned some valuable lessons, some of them from *you*—"

What those lessons were, he didn't get to say. For as the plane taxied to a stop, they could see Jessica waiting beside the Land Rover, waving.

On the way to the mission station, they passed one of Adam's irrigation projects—miles of lush green fields in vivid contrast to the nearby parched, barren land.

"Adam's work is invaluable," Jess asserted, with admiration. "It means the difference between starvation and survival for many people during the months when no rain falls."

Crystal could understand his pride in the projects. And why Jess had referred to him as a great humanitarian. There was much about Adam Sutherland to be admired.

"I would like to have visited the projects," she said sincerely.

"Yes, you would have appreciated them," he said distantly.

When they neared Salisbury, the conversation turned to David. Adam spoke optimistically about his condition and probable recovery.

A Rhodesian jet was being loaded with medical equipment when they landed. The three went directly to the big plane.

William and Clara Cliburn were standing to one side, directing David's move from an ambulance to the jet. Jess climbed aboard to tell Robert goodbye.

Then William stepped over to speak to Crystal. "David is conscious now, but we're keeping him heavily sedated for the trip. Robert won't tell David about his condition until after he's settled at Mission Hospital. It will take a while to know the extent of the damage. But it should be easier with David's family nearby." William smiled at Crystal. "And you, of course."

"I'll be there as long as he needs me," Crystal assured him.

"It's time to go," William said as he turned to supervise the last of the loading operation.

Just then, Jess came down the steps of the plane, but instead of coming over to speak to Crystal, she walked past, leaving Crystal and Adam to say their goodbyes.

Crystal stood rooted to the spot, Adam right behind her. It was time. She felt his hand on her arm. Turning, she looked up into his face.

"There are so many things I've refrained from saying to you, Crystal," he said. "And it hasn't been easy. But there's one thing I must tell you. I suppose you could call it a confession. There isn't much time," he said, glancing at the plane whose engines were roaring, sending a whoosh of exhaust on the ground below.

At the top of the steps, Robert was motioning for Crystal to board the plane. There wasn't much time.

"I'll hurry, Crystal," Adam promised. "I can't let you leave thinking I'm some kind of infidel. One reason I've helped the mission station is because I believe in the work they're doing . . . in what they're preaching. It's just that I've never taken the time to make a decision for myself, one way or the other. To accept it into my lifestyle." He shifted uncomfortably. "I've never admitted that to anyone."

"Adam," she said, smiling up at him. "That's not a sign of weakness, but of strength."

"The easy thing to do was ignore it, tell myself it wasn't all that important, as long as I knew what was in my heart. But now I know the importance of it. Had I possessed the kind of qualities David has," he said with a note of contrition in his voice, "perhaps I would have deserved a woman like you."

Crystal stared at him. "Adam," she whispered, just in case he meant what she hoped he meant, "sometimes we get a second chance."

"I'm going to hang on to that thought . . . just in case you're right."

The drums were throbbing once more, saying *Goodbye . . . goodbye . . . goodbye.* There wasn't time to tell him that knowing him had changed her life, that she wasn't in love with David Hamilton—

"Crys!" It was Robert again, calling her.

But Adam's eyes would not let her go. "Oh, Adam," she murmured, reaching up to touch his face. In that instant, as she tried to take a step forward, her foot struck his and she tripped, stumbling against him. Suddenly he was holding her, his hands in her hair. She opened her mouth to tell him she loved him, that she'd love him forever—

Just as she felt the soft fluttering of his breath against her lips, she felt a tug on her arm and heard Jess's voice saying they couldn't wait any longer. Crystal stepped away from his embrace, seeing the disappointment in his eyes.

"This time," he accused, as if she had committed a crime, "Kudsai was right!"

He turned and walked toward the airport without a backward glance.

"Adam!"

seventeen

"Adam!"

For a moment Crystal thought she must be dreaming! Even after three months, no detail of Adam Sutherland's handsome face had escaped her memory. But she certainly hadn't expected to run into him here in Switzerland, on this last leg of her trip back to Rhodesia.

"Th—they told me the flight was overbooked . . . that I'd have to move to the first class cabin, but—"

He stood, grinning, and motioned her to take the empty seat beside him. "Would you like to sit next to the window?" he asked. "I won't be looking out. Not as long as there's a beautiful blue-eyed blond next to me."

She plunked herself into the seat. "Well, what are *you* doing here? In Switzerland? At this time of night?"

"Escorting you to Africa," he said matter of factly. "Here, let me help you buckle up. There." He buckled his own seat belt, then halted her next question with a finger over her lips. "Shhh. The flight attendant must tell us about survival."

Impatiently, Crystal waited and looked out the window. The view was obscured by the clouds through which they were passing as the giant jet ascended to cruising altitude. But suddenly they were breaking through, skimming the clouds, now silvered by the large orb of the moon. "How beautiful," she said softly.

"Yes, isn't it?" But Adam's eyes were on her face, not on the impressive cloudscape through the window. "Now, let me tell you the reason I felt it necessary to meet you. My mother has faithfully practiced with her walker for three months now just to please you, and I couldn't run the risk of your getting sidetracked somewhere in the Alps."

It was almost impossible for Crystal to determine when a man with a British accent was joking or serious. "I don't know where you get these crazy ideas," she said in exasperation, and unfastened her seat belt.

"Jessica gave me the first clue," he informed her with a perfectly straight face. "But frankly, I didn't believe anyone could attract danger, and men, the way you do." He unfastened his belt and glanced in her direction.

"Oh, Adam," she began, wondering how to contradict such absurdities. Just then the flight attendant stopped to take their refreshment order.

"Coca Cola?" he asked and she nodded.

A warm feeling crept over her as she remembered the case of Coke he had bought to help her feel at home.

She sipped the drink, then attempted to explain herself. "Perhaps you still don't understand American humor. You see, the whole issue of men is a layover from our college days, when Jess tried to play matchmaker—" She groaned, realizing that another explanation was in order. "You'll just have to take my word for it, Adam, there have been very few men in my life."

Adam stared thoughtfully at his Coca Cola. "You're right about the humor," he agreed. "I don't see anything funny about it. It's quite obvious to me that you have a devastating effect on men. Look what happened to poor David. He jumped off a cliff because he thought you weren't in love with him."

Crystal darted him a sharp glance. "Who told you that?"

"Jessica."

Crystal shook her head. "Adam, David did *not* jump off a cliff. He *dived* off. He simply misjudged the depth of the water. It was a mistake, that's all."

"I understand he has completely recovered," Adam said with a lift in his voice, looking to her for confirmation.

"The fact that his spinal cord was dislocated, rather than severed, made all the difference. And William Cliburn was not being overly optimistic, as I had feared. David began to respond to treatment right away. He'll be fine."

"Prayer could have a lot to do with it too," Adam said soberly. "It seems everyone in Africa was praying for him."

"And I wouldn't be surprised if his nurse didn't play a part in his determination to get well as soon as possible."

Adam arched a brow. "Nurse?"

"Oh, I don't mean myself. David and his physical therapist fell in love almost immediately."

"But I thought he was in love with *you*."

Crystal frowned in reflection, wondering how to explain it. "David and I did love each other," she admitted. "There was something very special between us. Maybe because we had a preconceived idea of what our ideal mate would be, and it seemed each of us met that ideal for the other." She sighed. "But it didn't take long for David to decide I wasn't the one for him."

Adam cut his eyes around at her. "Why not?"

"Well," she admitted uncomfortably, "I think David wants a more settled way of life than he would have with me. I mean, unusual things *do* seem to happen with me around—"

"Ah, ha!" Adam said forcefully and she saw a few heads

turn in their direction. "So you're beginning to acknowledge it. You *are* a most intriguing personality, you know."

"Oh, Adam, there is absolutely nothing to Jess's intrigue
theory. Why, in all of Africa, only one man was ever
interested in me, and that turned out to be nothing more
than friendship."

"You're wrong," Adam replied softly.

She turned her face toward him and studied his profile.
It told her nothing. What did he mean? She cleared her
throat. "Where is . . . Elise?"

She noticed that other passengers were turning out their
overhead lights, as if getting ready for the night.

"She took my advice," Adam replied, removing his
suitcoat and laying it on an empty seat across the aisle. "I
told her that marriage was not something to take lightly.
When two people love each other enough to marry, they
should make every effort to resolve their differences.
Besides," he added, after loosening his tie, "there is room
for only one blond in my life. By the way, why are you
returning to Africa?"

"To see Jess . . . and your mother," she replied.

He reached overhead and turned out the small light. The
cabin was dark except for the slivers of moonlight filtering
through the window. A bed of clouds floated beneath
them.

"Are you sure?" he asked quietly.

"No," she whispered, ducking her head, "not exactly."
Her hair, silvery in the moon's rays, fell forward around
her face.

Adam lifted her chin with his fingers until she was
looking at him. His dark blue eyes, now warm and placid
as the sea, held glints of light. He spoke quietly, in rhythm

with the hum of the engine, lulling other passengers to
sleep. "Do you remember when you were at the estate, and
mentioned hearing the drums?"

She nodded.

"Do you know what my mother says about the drums?"

A light began to dance in her eyes, and her cheeks
dimpled. "Voodoo?" she asked with feigned innocence.

He gave her a look of reprimand, but his lips curved in
a smile. "That wasn't what I meant . . . and I think you
know it. But I'll have to admit I was concerned when Bari
put that doll on your pillow. With all the other counts
against me, I didn't need a hex, too."

"Oh, Adam," she breathed, watching his face so close to
hers, "I didn't want to fall in love with you. I
couldn't . . . not with all the differences between us."

"And I felt so helpless to do anything to persuade you,"
he said. "I knew you wouldn't be swayed by the estate and
everything I own. And I knew I didn't exemplify those
solid spiritual convictions you'd found in David. I thought
it was hopeless, so I just tried not to interfere. Until the
accident—"

"I know. I guess I've seen too much. But a relationship
between a man and a woman that is not based on God's
kind of love is doomed to fail. Besides, Jess said you were
looking for a replacement for Elise, and when she came
back—"

"Not so." He stopped her words with his lips. Nothing
else seemed to matter in that moment but the warmth and
strength of his arms, the yielding of her lips to his.

"Adam," she breathed against his ear when he reluctantly withdrew his lips and laid his cheek against hers.
"Regardless of what you may think, or what Jessica has

said, I've never felt this way about any man."

He drew a shaky breath. "Marry me? Right away?"

"Yes," she replied immediately. "And Jess was right about something else."

Adam moved away only slightly. "About what?"

"About you, Adam. She said I should be careful. For I might find you irresistible."

He smiled. "Two days, Miss Janis," he said in a mocking threat. "Two days . . . or however long it takes to get a marriage license." Then he closed his eyes.

Crystal leaned against him, too exhilarated to sleep. Soon, beneath the canopy of clouds, the Dark Continent would come into view. But Africa was no longer dark and forbidding. It was green with promise, nurtured by Adam's irrigation project and their mutual faith.

Already she could hear the drums of Shelomoh, beating out the message of their love—*forever, forever, forever.*

A Letter To Our Readers

Dear Reader:

In order that we might better contribute to your reading enjoyment, we would appreciate your taking a few minutes to respond to the following questions. When completed, please return to the following:

Karen Carroll, Editor
Heartsong Presents
P.O. Box 719
Uhrichsville, Ohio 44683

1. Did you enjoy reading *Drums of Shelomah*?
   ☐ Very much. I would like to see more books
      by this author!
   ☐ Moderately
      I would have enjoyed it more if _____

   _____

2. Are you a member of *Heartsong Presents*? Yes   No
   If no, where did you purchase this book? _____

   _____

3. What influenced your decision to purchase
   this book? (Circle those that apply.)

Cover	Back cover copy
Title	Friends
Publicity	Other _____

4. On a scale from 1 (poor) to 10 (superior), please rate the following elements.

___Heroine   ___Plot

___Hero   ___Inspirational theme

___Setting   ___Secondary characters

5. What settings would you like to see covered in *Heartsong Presents* books?

_____

_____

6. What are some inspirational themes you would like to see treated in future books?_____

_____

_____

7. Would you be interested in reading other *Heartsong Presents* titles?   Yes   No

8. Please circle your age range:

Under 18	18-24	25-34
35-45	46-55	Over 55

9. How many hours per week do you read? _____

Name _____

Occupation _____

Address _____

City _____ State _____ Zip _____

HEARTSONG PRESENTS books are inspirational romances in contemporary and historical settings, designed to give you an enjoyable, spirit-lifting reading experience.

AVAILABLE NOW AT A SALE PRICE OF $2.95 each!

____HP 1 A TORCH FOR TRINITY, *Colleen L. Reece*
____HP 2 WILDFLOWER HARVEST, *Colleen L. Reece*
____HP 3 RESTORE THE JOY, *Sara Mitchell*
____HP 4 REFLECTIONS OF THE HEART, *Sally Laity*
____HP 5 THIS TREMBLING CUP, *Marlene Chase*
____HP 6 THE OTHER SIDE OF SILENCE, *Marlene Chase*
____HP 7 CANDLESHINE, *Colleen L. Reece*
____HP 8 DESERT ROSE, *Colleen L. Reece*
____HP 9 HEARTSTRINGS, *Irene B. Brand*
____HP10 SONG OF LAUGHTER, *Lauraine Snelling*
____HP11 RIVER OF FIRE, *Jacquelyn Cook*
____HP12 COTTONWOOD DREAMS, *Norene Morris*
____HP13 PASSAGE OF THE HEART, *Kjersti Hoff Baez*
____HP14 A MATTER OF CHOICE, *Susannah Hayden*
____HP15 WHISPERS ON THE WIND, *Maryn Langer*
____HP16 SILENCE IN THE SAGE, *Colleen L. Reece*
____HP17 LLAMA LADY, *VeraLee Wiggins*
____HP18 ESCORT HOMEWARD, *Eileen M. Berger*
____HP19 A PLACE TO BELONG, *Janelle Jamison*
____HP20 SHORES OF PROMISE, *Kate Blackwell*
____HP21 GENTLE PERSUASION, *Veda Boyd Jones*
____HP22 INDY GIRL, *Brenda Bancroft*
____HP23 GONE WEST, *Kathleen Karr*
____HP24 WHISPERS IN THE WILDERNESS, *Colleen L. Reece*
____HP25 REBAR, *Mary Carpenter Reid*
____HP26 MOUNTAIN HOUSE, *Mary Louise Colln*
____HP27 BEYOND THE SEARCHING RIVER, *Jacquelyn Cook*
____HP28 DAKOTA DAWN, *Lauraine Snelling*
____HP29 FROM THE HEART, *Sara Mitchell*
____HP30 A LOVE MEANT TO BE, *Brenda Bancroft*
____HP31 DREAM SPINNER, *Sally Laity*
____HP32 THE PROMISED LAND, *Kathleen Karr*
____HP33 SWEET SHELTER, *VeraLee Wiggins*
____HP34 UNDER A TEXAS SKY, *Veda Boyd Jones*
____HP35 WHEN COMES THE DAWN, *Brenda Bancroft*
____HP36 THE SURE PROMISE, *JoAnn A. Grote*
____HP37 DRUMS OF SHELOMOH, *Yvonne Lehman*
____HP38 A PLACE TO CALL HOME, *Eileen M. Berger*
____HP39 RAINBOW HARVEST, *Norene Morris*
____HP40 PERFECT LOVE, *Janelle Jamison*

ABOVE TITLES ARE REGULARLY PRICED AT $4.95! USE THE ORDER FORM BELOW AND YOU PAY ONLY $2.95 per book

SEND TO: Heartsong Presents Reader's Service
P.O. Box 719, Uhrichsville, Ohio 44683

Please send me the items checked above. I am enclosing $_____ (please add $1.00 to cover postage per order). Send check or money order, no cash or C.O.D.s, please.

To place a credit card order, call 1-800-847-8270.

NAME_____

ADDRESS_____

CITY/STATE_____ ZIP_____

HPS JULY

add a little MYSTERY to your romance!

TWO GREAT INSPIRATIONAL ROMANCES WITH JUST A TOUCH OF MYSTERY
BY MARLENE J. CHASE

_____*The Other Side of Silence*—Anna Durham finds a purpose for living in the eyes of a needy child and a reason to love in the eyes of a lonely physician...but first the silence of secrets must be broken. HP6 BHSB-07 $2.95.

_____*This Trembling Cup*— A respite on a plush Wisconsin resort may just be the thing for Angie Carlson's burn-out—or just the beginning of a devious plot unraveling and the promise of love. HP5 BHSB-05 $2.95.

Send to: Heartsong Presents Reader's Service
P.O. Box 719
Uhrichsville, Ohio 44683

Please send me the items checked above. I am enclosing $_____(please add $1.00 to cover postage and handling per order).
Send check or money order, no cash or C.O.D.s, please.
   To place a credit card order, call 1-800-847-8270.

NAME_____

ADDRESS _____

CITY/STATE _____ ZIP_____
CHASE

Inspirational Romance at its Best from one of America's Favorite Authors!

FOUR HISTORICAL ROMANCES
BY COLLEEN L. REECE

___ *A Torch for Trinity*—When Trinity Mason sacrifices her teaching ambitions for a one-room school, her life—and Will Thatcher's—will never be the same. HP1 BHSB-01 $2.95

___ *Candleshine*-A sequel to *A Torch for Trinity*—With the onslaught of World War II, Candleshine Thatcher dedicates her life to nursing, and then her heart to a brave Marine lieutenant. HP7 BHSB-06 $2.95

___ *Wildflower Harvest*—Ivy Ann and Laurel were often mistaken for each other...was it too late to tell one man the truth? HP2 BHSB-02 $2.95

___ *Desert Rose*-A sequel to *Wildflower Harvest*—When Rose Birchfield falls in love with one of Michael's letters, and then with a cowboy named Mike, no one is more confused than Rose herself. HP8 BHSB-08 $2.95

Send to: Heartsong Presents Reader's Service
P.O. Box 719
Uhrichsville, Ohio 44683

Please send me the items checked above. I am enclosing
$_____(please add $1.00 to cover postage and handling per order).
Send check or money order, no cash or C.O.D.s, please.
   To place a credit card order, call 1-800-847-8270.

NAME_____

ADDRESS _____

CITY/STATE _____ ZIP_____

REECE

LOVE A GREAT LOVE STORY?

Introducing Heartsong Presents —
Your Inspirational Book Club

Heartsong Presents Christian romance reader's service will provide you with four never before published romance titles every month! In fact, your books will be mailed to you at the same time advance copies are sent to book reviewers. You'll preview each of these new and unabridged books before they are released to the general public.

These books are filled with the kind of stories you have been longing for—stories of courtship, chivalry, honor, and virtue. Strong characters and riveting plot lines will make you want to read on and on. Romance is not dead, and each of these romantic tales will remind you that Christian faith is still the vital ingredient in an intimate relationship filled with true love and honest devotion.

Sign up today to receive your first set. Send no money now. We'll bill you only $9.97 post-paid with your shipment. Then every month you'll automatically receive the latest four "hot off the press" titles for the same low post-paid price of $9.97. That's a savings of 50% off the $4.95 cover price. When you consider the exaggerated shipping charges of other book clubs, your savings are even greater!

THERE IS NO RISK—you may cancel at any time without obligation. And if you aren't completely satisfied with any selection, return it for an immediate refund.

TO JOIN, just complete the coupon below, mail it today, and get ready for hours of wholesome entertainment.

Now you can curl up, relax, and enjoy some great reading full of the warmhearted spirit of romance.

— — —Curl up with Heartsong!— — —

YES! Sign me up for Heartsong!

NEW MEMBERSHIPS WILL BE SHIPPED IMMEDIATELY!
Send no money now. We'll bill you only $9.97 post-paid with your first shipment of four books. Or for faster action, call toll free 1-800-847-8270.

NAME _____

ADDRESS _____

CITY _____ STATE / ZIP _____

MAIL TO: HEARTSONG / P.O. Box 719 Uhrichsville, Ohio 44683
YES II